Angels of Protection;

True Angel Stories in the Modern Age

ISBN: 978-0-9827877-2-4

Published by:
Creative House International Press, Inc.
CreativeHousePress.com

Publisher's Note

It is with great joy that I am able to present this book of wonderful art, and stories that relate to Angels-also known as Spirit Guides. Each story has a special meaning, and I hope it gives you, the reader, an opportunity to open yourself to new possibilities in awareness, or helps you deal with a moment in your own life.

If you have a story that you would like to share with us, please feel free to email us at: Angels@CreativeHousePress.com. Angela and Robert will be reviewing stories for future collections.

We would also like to encourage you to visit our web site at: CreativeHousePress.com/Angels.htm to learn more about the people who share their stories with us.

May the Angels watch over you,
B. Alan Bourgeois
Publisher
Creative House International Press, Inc.

Angela would like to dedicate this book to: God, my boyfriend, my publisher, editor, co-author, contributing writers to this book and my cat, Tiger.

Rob would like to dedicate this book to:
God, my Guru, my spiritual path, the Angels, my wife, my sons, my family, my friends, my co-author and publisher, the hungry, the homeless, the poor,
the abused, the innocent victims of all wars, the oceans and rivers, the land, the healers, the departed, and all those on the road.

Table of Contents

All Angel introductions are written by Rob Jacobs

HOW THE ANGEL PROJECT CAME ABOUT

Angela Taylor

A few years back, around 2007, I had this intuitive feeling to get in touch with a friend I had known for approximately twenty-five years, Rob Jacobs, an artist living in the Los Angeles area. We had initially met at a spiritual convocation, sponsored by our church.

I remembered that Rob was a person who had gone through difficult health issues, in the physical and emotional areas, and how, through the help of two very knowledgeable, compassionate healers, had largely resolved them.

I was experiencing something quite similar. As we connected and spoke about health issues we also got caught up with what each other had been doing. Rob was working on a series of art, which he called **Angels of Protection**. I was intrigued and moved by the experience Rob related to me which had to do with his father, Harry, and how Harry's life was spared by an angelic message, which is told in Rob's angel story, included in this book. The artwork behind this extraordinary experience is Rob's **Angel 5 / Of My Father**.

In a synchronistic way I began relating to Rob some of the angel stories and experiences from friends. As we were talking, it seemed that a lot of Rob's angel art resonated with me on emotional, mental and spiritual levels and the idea came up of combining the angel stories, (stories of angelic protection experienced by the many people throughout the world), with Rob's art series, which presently has sixteen images, fourteen which are included in this book.

In a world filled with violence, natural catastrophes, financial concerns, wars, and fear, Rob and I felt that a book of true angel stories would be a flash of positive light to the public, and help to inspire others that angels are real, and all we have to do is have faith in that reality of protection, love and joy.

Some areas of angelic protection in this book, include: of animals, in time of war, of mothers, of fathers, of children, in the world of danger, in areas of money, finance and business, of the rivers and oceans, on the road, of health, and of overall protective blessings.

Lastly, we often think of angels as wonderful luminous beings of love, compassion and protection, and these stories show those qualities. However, one of the most inspiring areas in partaking of them, are the examples of those often "the protected" - our relatives, the animals, even strangers – rise up to the ultimate consciousness, and, in a world of duality, they, themselves, become angels of protection.

Rob and I thank our publisher, Alan Bourgeois at Creative House Press, for all his help, and for his faith in our angel project.

HOW OUR ANGEL BOOK DIFFERS FROM OTHERS

Rob Jacobs

The Passover Seder is a Jewish ritual feast that marks the beginning of the Jewish holiday of Passover. During the holiday the Jewish people, at the Seder, ask, "why is this night different from all other nights?" In many ways this question is as interesting as the answers.

In world history, the 'how' and 'why' questions have been asked billions of times.

Someone once said, and I quote, 'the best philosophy final exam he ever heard of asked one question: Why? Most of the class wrote furiously for two hours. One guy got an 'A.' His answer was, why not?' Probably the person who received a 'B' answered, "because."

So, ***how*** is **Angels of Protection / True Angel Stories in the Modern Age** different from other angel books?

This book is a compilation of true stories/experiences that take place during the middle to late twentieth century, from REAL people, revolving around different forms of angelic protection. These can range from protection in time of war to the rescue of a child in the backyard swimming pool. The question here is what does the word 'true' mean? And, an interesting philosophical discussion could follow. Does the word 'true' have the same connotation as the word, 'fact,' for example? Let me attempt to respond to this issue. A fact is a statement that can be proved, for example, "I have five fingers on my right hand." In our system of counting, and in the English language, that is a statement of fact. However, here the word 'true,' has a slightly different connotation. It means, 'a sincere, reliable, accurate rendering of an experience.' Every story is told exactly as it happened. Can the stories be 'proven?' Dear reader, possibly not to you, but absolutely to the authors who experienced the related events. Some names and locations have been changed. Along with these stories, reproduced are fourteen of the sixteen images from my art series, **Angels of Protection** (http://www.angelsofprotection.com), whose individual titles relate to them.

One thing our book does not do is to address the question: what or who are angels? It also does not go into the history of the known angels, like Michael or Gabriel, or the whole angel phenomenon. This has been done by numerous books before ours, and, from my readings, rendered in very beautiful and inspiring ways.

Our purpose is to present the angel experience, the stories and art, and to respect the reader, that he or she, in the reading process, will have their own experiences and feelings. Some of these may be discharged in laughter, feelings of joy and love, and possibly sadness. A few tears may be shed, just as I have in partaking of some of these magical episodes.

11:45pm. In one of the toughest neighborhoods in the world, a man walks down a rain soaked sidewalk. He has no wings. He wears a suit and tie

2:33am. Another city, same time, and a dark brown sky of danger. This being wears wings, and his face is a flash of off-white. He is also wearing a suit and tie, and is archived on canvas. The sound and power of lightening is heard and seen in the distance.

Two beings. Both protectors. Both angels. Both - **Angels of Protection.**

Angels of Protection

True Angel Stories in the Modern Age

WRITTEN & COMPILED BY

Angela Taylor & Rob Jacobs

Angel 10/On The Road

There is always the possibility of danger on the road, from mechanical failure to people who do not have love in their hearts. In this arena of white paint, the road runs diagonally behind the angel's head, behind his red wings, and off the picture plane, into infinity. And another road (top half of the picture) culminates in a snake's head - danger. The predominant color - red, is symbolic of the blood of life and death, and being the color of the angel's wings, provides assurance that this angel will protect all, in this physical environment, and on the road.

A BRIDGE OF MERCY

Tom White

I remember that I was working late one night at the factory where I was lead on the second shift, and the weather had turned cold and icy. It was one of those typical Oklahoma ice storms that seem to do its worst to make sure no vehicle was safe, and that those things that we take for granted, such as light and heat, are taken away in the time it takes a ton of ice to snap a power line.

My wife drove in to pick me up since we were only a one-car family at the time and we took our usual route home. The usual route included a twisting piece of interstate that was elevated above the surrounding city for about a mile. This lovely piece of road is known by the locals as Belle Isle Bridge and it's famous for the damage that its icy pavement inflicts upon people and the cars they drive.

As I was just getting ready to drive up onto the bridge I noticed my wife was praying, I asked her why? She said that she "Wanted help getting across the bridge safely." I kind of scoffed and told her that it wasn't a problem. I could handle the bridge. I barely got that sentence out of my mouth when we rounded a section of the road where there were three vehicles that had collided in an icy crash. I stopped our car and got out. I told my wife to pull on down the bridge away from the accident.

Two smaller cars, smoke emitting from them, had slid down to the lower edge of the bridge and were just sitting there. An African-American male was sitting in the front car and he was already on his cell phone. Who knows, he may have been on it when the accident happened. The vehicle just behind his contained a young Asian couple who appeared to be in shock. The third vehicle was in the middle of the bridge facing the wrong way with a middle aged female sitting in the driver's seat of her Suburban, her door crushed and she appeared to be trapped inside. I checked on everyone in the first two vehicles and they seemed to be okay. I then went out to the woman's vehicle in the middle of the road. The air was filled with the smell of alcohol and gasoline. She was crying that she could not get out of her vehicle. I took the door and (don't ask me how; I still don't know to this day) ripped it off its hinges. I helped her out of the car and walked her down and put her in our car with my wife.

That's not the end of this story, while I was back up helping the others involved in the accident I noticed that there was an 18 wheeler coming up the bridge at a pretty good clip. I cleared the people back to the side and just hoped he had enough space to get around the vehicle sitting in the middle of the bridge facing the wrong direction. As soon as that trucker saw it he locked his brakes and that huge truck just seemed to shiver under the weight of its momentum being slowed. The truck made it past the car in the middle and I watched it as the entire truck slid past us and then began to swerve toward the right hand side of the road. He was heading directly toward my car that had my wife and the woman from the accident sitting inside like pins in a bowling alley. My heart seemed to stop and time seemed to crawl as this truck continued its slide. I immediately prayed for protection for my wife. It was quick, but no sooner than the words were out of my mouth, with the truck only feet away from my wife, something happened. It would later be explained that the trucks axle just snapped and caused the truck to immediately swerve back to the left long enough to pass my car, my wife and the twice blessed woman, then it swerved back to the right and came to a halt at the base of the bridge.

Words cannot express the tenseness of that moment or the relief of the deliverance. You may have some really valid and logical explanations for what happened on that icy Belle Isle Bridge that evening, but as for me and my family…well, we choose a more angelic explanation.

SILENCE ON THE ROAD

Anonymous

Much of the following story is about my grandson, Patrick, when he was about four years old. He is seventeen now. One day he and his younger brother were with their paternal grandmother, Dixie, traveling from Lancaster, California, out west to Green Valley. All of a sudden, while using an infrequently traveled back road, the car developed a flat tire. As I said this was in the middle of "nowhere". So, there Dixie is, no cell phone, and with two small kids in the car. Patrick's brother, Cody was only two years old at the time and was sleeping soundly in the back seat.

There was a small hill on the road and Dixie noticed a very old pick-up truck coming toward them. The truck stopped near them, and a somewhat "scruffy looking" man got out, saw the situation and proceeded to change the tire. Of course Dixie was concerned. Here they were, out in the country, with this man. Even stranger, Patrick, who was by nature on the quiet side, especially with strangers, began talking to this man, asking questions, etc. Dixie said this fellow never said a word, would just smile and pat Patrick on the head. After changing the tire, the fellow got back in his pick-up, and went back the same way he came. That was the interesting thing. He did not continue on in the direction he was traveling, but turned around and went back from where he had come, as if he had come only to help the family.

Dixie felt comfortable enough then to ask Patrick if he knew the fellow since he was so talkative. Patrick said, "No, I don't know him. He was an angel." I wish Dixie was still with us. I'm sure she could elaborate and make this true angel story even more interesting. Remembering how cautious Patrick was, as I said, especially with people he didn't know, I believe they had a true “angel encounter”. Praise God for them.

WALL OF PROTECTION

Glenda K. Rodger

On at least three occasions it seems my dad had become my guardian angel, the first just shortly after he passed. I was on my way to work, as always running a little late, and my mind going in a hundred different directions. My commute of twenty-five miles took me on a busy highway and through a small rural town in California. I could have taken the freeway but I find the tranquility of the old back roads more relaxing and beautifully scenic. I had slowed to the 35mph speed limit, passed through the downtown section of Rosamond, and was just beginning to accelerate as I was exiting town. To my horror, I looked at a black, old rusty pickup truck coming towards me. The driver was apparently unable to steer and make the turn. I could not look directly at him. In my peripheral vision I saw his truck, and his left hood corner was within a few inches of my driver's side door. I prepared to die. In the next second I felt my car shift slightly to the right as a protective wall had come down between my door and the front of this old pickup truck. I was shaking so badly I pulled off onto the right shoulder of the road. I did not know exactly what had happened. For a few seconds I think I believed I was dead. After a few minutes I realized not only was I very much alive, neither my car, nor my body, had even so much as a scratch.

About a year or so later I was once again driving when it came time to navigate a railroad crossing. I always look both ways but this day my mind must have been somewhere else. I proceeded through the crossing; the crossing guards were not down, no red lights blinking and as soon as I was over the first rail I heard the most horrendous, unbelievably loud horn. I looked to my right to see a train very close and coming towards me at what seemed, at the time, to be lightening fast. I felt a push from behind and, once again a protective wall, out of nowhere, had inserted itself between the train and my car.

Many years passed. By this time I had a little daughter and my mother lived with us. One day we were all in Lancaster, a California High Desert town, for a 'fun day of shopping.' We would always refer to these trips as "girl's day out." We had just had one of our favorite lunches ('drive-thru' only for the girls), and afterwards were merrily heading down a four-lane road. We were in the lane closest to the sidewalk when I noticed an older sedan pulling out. It did not look as if it was going to stop, but sure enough, it did come to a stop directly in front of us. I was too close to prevent hitting it. Time stood still, frozen, and I could hear my dad telling me, "Glen you're going to have a collision, aim your driver's corner between the man's backseat and gas tank. If you hit the car straight everyone will get hurt. If you plough into his door he may get killed. If you angel the car with the passenger side of the hood ramming his car both mom and the baby could be hurt badly."

Dad's words were very clear and it seemed like I had all the time in the world to follow his advice. We did indeed collide and no one was seriously hurt. This time Dad's angelic protective wall just froze time so he could walk me through this experience, on the road.

A DATE WITH A SEMI

Marysue Rivera

When my daughter was in grade school, I rode along with two other mothers for a school field trip to the zoo. The field trip was very enjoyable and I loved sharing this experience with my daughter and her class. Before arriving, however, we could see that major construction was taking place for a new freeway, and that getting into the zoo was quite a difficult process.

After the field trip, and on our way home, the mother driving was going to make a left turn heading back the way we came to the zoo. I was sitting in the back seat of her car. The mother driving decided, for some unknown reason, to try to make her planned left hand turn as a giant semi was speeding close towards us. When she pulled out she ended up being right in front of a semi hauling two trailers filled with tons of dirt from the dig for the freeway. It was a driving misjudgment call on her part, like trying to cross the tracks in the hope of beating a speeding train.

The next thing I remember was the semi was right at the side of the car on the driver's side. The sound of the engine, and size of the semi, became the most frightening moment of my life. But, what took place then was almost unbelievable. I had this feeling of incredible peace. Every thing around me became a soft blur. I couldn't see out of it. That moment in time was peaceful bliss. I thought, "I am dead." I was not afraid. I felt completely at peace, completely fulfilled. It was nothing I had ever felt before. I tried to see out of the soft like-blur around me. Then the next thing I remember is being back where I was, in the back seat of the car. The car was at a dead stop in the lane, but on the other side of where the semi was and facing west. I looked out the back window and saw the back of the semi trailer and the dust of the semi whirling behind us. The two other mothers, and I, were trying to catch our breath and were looking at each other, stunned. We then started to cry and grabbed onto each other's hands with having a clear memory of what just happened with the semi on top of us in the car.

The first words that came out of all our mouths, and almost at the same time was, "We were saved by our guardian angels." We should have been dead. There was no chance we were going to survive a cash like we had just experienced, in a small car, with a semi speeding toward us, carrying two trailers filled with tons of dirt.

What happened that day was unexplainable, unexplainable, except it happened. For me, personally, it was my guardian angel, in my blissful state, that saved us from leaving the planet at that present moment in time.

HOPE LIVES AMONG THE WRECKAGE

Tom White

Do you remember the story that I told you about the Belle Isle Bridge? This bridge must be someplace special because I think that my angel must hang out there, waiting for me to come along.

This story takes place in the springtime, no ice to worry about. I was driving our new Mercury van that we, as a family, just loved to death. Two captain seats up front, two in the middle and a bench in the back. It really fit our family well. It ran like a cheetah and purred like a kitten. Who could ask for more? Anyway, I was working extremely late due to the fact that I was lead on the 2nd shift and then I stayed late to use the computer to write articles for the company newsletter. I was one of the original members of the Editorial Committee and one of the few who got a kick out of writing. So, needless to say, I contributed quite a bit. I finished what I could and was heading home at about 2am. On the way I had to cross the Belle Isle Bridge which to explain to the un-initiated is about a mile of curving, elevated interstate set in the heart of Oklahoma City.

While I was driving over it, minding my own business, singing along with an oldies station, I cast a glance in my rear view mirror and noticed that there was a car coming up behind me way too fast. The vehicle was swerving in and out of what little traffic there was at 2am. I looked back down to make sure that he had room to go around me. Now, those of you who have been in a high speed crash will probably understand this better than others. I barely had time to finish that last thought when this car hit me from behind. I was hit with such force that the back of the van was blown open and forced into a spin. At the moment of impact I was thrown backward so hard that I immediately broke the captain seat I was sitting in. I continued backwards, out of my seatbelt and to the right, as the van continued to spin. I struck the middle passenger side captain seat and snapped it backwards. I crashed into the bench seat and in that moment, this one isolated moment, I noticed that the world was spinning by through a huge, gaping hole where the rear of the van used to be.

Out of my mouth came three words, words that came from a heart that was pretty convinced that I was dead or soon to be. Three words; I don't know if I screamed them, thought them or just spoke them, but I do know that I have never meant a prayer as much as I meant that one. "GOD HELP ME!" That was it. That was all I could get out before the van went nose first into a concrete retaining wall. I laid there for a moment before I realized that it was over.

As I lay there I checked for broken parts and realized that I needed to get out of the van. What used to be the tail end of the van was hanging out in the lanes of traffic and I couldn't get out that way. The side door was crushed to the point that it could not be opened, as was the passenger front door. That left me with the way I had got in not more than fifteen minutes before, the driver's side front door. I crawled back through the twisted van and had to kick the door open. I got out just as a few motorists who had stopped came up to see if I was all right. The car that had hit me had been thrown three lanes over onto an entry ramp. It had to jump a three-foot concrete barrier to get there. The young man who was driving had a cut on his forehead but otherwise was okay. I sat down, mostly because I couldn't stand anymore, and waited for the emergency vehicles to arrive. When they arrived one of the EMTs came over to me, looked at the van and then at me. "Who pulled you out?" he asked. "No one," I said, "I got out myself." The EMT looked at me and said, "I've been doing this for ten years and I have never seen someone live through an accident like this, let alone walk away from it."

But walk away I did, a little stressed, but not injured, muscles sore but not broken. The van was destroyed but I was delivered.

Thank God.

Angel 9/In the World of Danger

At this time in 2010, it has been reported that approximately one hundred wars are being waged in the world. Drug cartels are engaged in violence against armies of their own countries, human beings are murdered for a few dollars, and yet, every day, men, women, children and animals are protected by the Messengers of God as they experience life in a world of danger.

There are three main elements in the angel image: Two grotesque figures floating in the blue sky and in the foreground the dominant angel standing beside us in a mode of love, courage and protection.

DO NOT WALK ON THE GLASS

Anonymous

I was supposed to pick up Scott, Ray's and my son, from a music lesson at 2:00pm. I took a nap and as I awoke a bit late, ran to the car barefooted. I then had this intuitive feeling/thought: "Get your shoes!" I thought, 'oh, that is silly,' and kept going to the car. Then it was a bit stronger – **"Get your shoes!"** I thought 'fine,' and ran and got them; I didn't put them on but threw them in the back seat.

On the way to the lesson I was rear ended on the freeway and there was glass everywhere. If I hadn't had those shoes my feet would have been cut by glass when I got out of the car. I was so fortunate to have listened to that angelic intuition, and fortunate, also, that angel had been so pushy. Most fortunate, no one was seriously hurt.

SAVED BY A QUEEN

Ruth Aroni

Not too long ago, I was driving down Ventura Boulevard, on a Monday evening, in the Encino area. For those of you not familiar with the Los Angeles area, Encino is in the San Fernando Valley, just "over the hill," as they say, from Hollywood and West Los Angeles. Ventura Boulevard is the main street of the San Fernando Valley, as Wilshire Boulevard would be in Los Angeles, or Sunset Boulevard running through West Hollywood.

Suddenly a car in front of me came to an abrupt halt. I hit the brakes as hard as I could, and stopped inches short of a collision. You can imagine the degree of relief I felt, and thanked the universe for interfering in a potential disaster.

Immediately after the light changed, another car crossed in front of me. The license plate on this vehicle did not have random numbers or letters, just the name 'Malca,' which means 'queen' in Hebrew. There must be at least eight to ten million cars in the Los Angeles area, and a license plate with an unusual name passes in front of me, after I had been protected from what could have been a very nasty accident.

Malca happens to be my Mother's first name. I knew her spirit had interceded for me in this near collision, and I am eternally grateful to that

Angel Mother who protected me, from near disaster, on a Monday evening.

A DAY UNLIKE ANY OTHER

Anonymous

It was a day like any other, what I would call a 'normal day.' I had to go out to do some errands, take care of business, and with my daughter by my side, was driving through a business park that I had driven through many times before. The road here had extreme curves, and I had always made a mental evaluation that the area was a somewhat dangerous place to drive. However, I had driven through many times in the past, and it was just an area I had to go through to get to where I was going – nothing more, nothing less.

However, on this day I was full of fear. Where does this come from – this intuitive feeling? My daughter and I both felt that we needed to pray for protection, immediately! The curves in the street were flat, not 'cliff like,' but, as I said, still they were extreme, and seemed to loom up very fast and furiously.

As we prayed, we felt some peace and then, within a minute or two, a HUGE, HUMONGOUS truck missed smashing our small Saturn car. I knew right then and there an Angel of Protection, sent from the Lord himself, had saved us from a certain death.

There is no doubt, whatsoever, in my mind, heart and soul that angels exist. I am sure of this. In a moment of extraordinary danger, one interfered, and we lived to tell the story.

I pray now whenever I leave the house, to drive - anywhere.

RUNNING FOR MY LIFE

Josh Villarrial

My name is Josh Villarrial. September 4, 2009, was just another night at work for me as a security guard at the Visalia Holiday Inn, doing my normal rounds, checking out the inside of the hotel and the outside perimeter, making sure there was nothing unusual going on. At one point, I noticed a couple with a baby standing outside the hotel. They seemed to be in a heated discussion so I thought I would just go up and see if they needed any help. I asked them if there was anything that I could do to help out, they said, "No thanks." I walked away but kept an eye on them to make sure nothing got out of hand in case I needed to call for backup, but I kept my distance. Everything seemed to calm down. They went their way and everything was back to normal, so I thought. About an hour or two later came my dinner break. The night was nice out so I got a book out of the car, and for some unknown reason, something I never do, left my flashlight and pepper spray sitting on the front seat. I stood leaning on the outside of my car and reading my book when all of a sudden this guy approached me out of nowhere, and before I knew what was happening, he was right up in my face yelling at me saying, "You're the one I'm looking for. Yeah, you're him!"

He then grabbed my two-way radio, threw it, and started to raise his right hand up in the air. In his hand was a huge knife and it came down hard in an attempt to stab me, to kill me, but I was able to block the first attack. We then started scuffling around and all I knew, at this point, was that I was fighting for my life. As I said, this guy was out to kill me. A person I didn't know, had never seen, had, as his sole purpose at this moment in time, to end my life. He kept saying over and over, "I am doing this for me and my father the devil." He looked like he was possessed with some kind of evil entity, so evil that all I could feel was this massive negative energy. It was so awful that I, at this point, truly did not know if I was going to survive the night.

All of a sudden, the energy completely changed, and I felt the presence of an angel sent from God. The presence was so great it literally pulled the two of us apart so that I could run and get away from this crazed man. It was like two invisible hands reached down, and bam! We were apart!

I ran to the first door possible, and believe it or not, I still had the book in my hand, which had the key card that opened all the doors of the hotel. I got the key card out of the book, opened that door and ran inside to the first room I could find; unlocked the door, got inside and looked behind me to see if the crazed person was there and thank God, he wasn't. I got to the telephone and called 911 and that's when I noticed that I had blood all over my shirt. I had been stabbed during the scuffle and didn't even realize it. I was in shock but the 911 Operator kept talking to me and I told her that there was a woman working the front desk, and I didn't know if the man had also attacked her. I put the 911 Operator on hold for a moment and tried to reach the front desk to warn Loraine, the front desk clerk, but she didn't answer her phone. Obviously, I knew something was wrong. I got back on line with the 911 Operator and told her to have the officers to first check on Loraine.

Loraine was in bad shape in the security room next to the front desk; she had been stabbed eighteen times, all over her body, including her spine and head. She was airlifted to Fresno due to her condition being so severe. The emergency people then took me to Kaweah Delta Hospital by ambulance. I had been stabbed three times, once in my left upper torso and twice in my left arm. The staff at the hospital checked me out to make sure that I didn't have any life threatening issues. They also did a cat scan, stitched up my wounds, and sent me home after a few hours. My parents and my older brother Eric were there, and I cannot explain adequately the impact that, that love, from my family, had in a time of such a life crisis.

Well, I've told my story. I believe in Angels with all my heart and have no doubt that they are here with us, and come in to help us in times of need. They are awesome and so wonderful, and sent by God to help people all around the world at different moments.

I am still going through post-traumatic syndrome and therapy to help me get through the horrific experience, that, for some karmic reason I had to go through, and, although I have relayed the story here, I still have a very difficult time talking about it. At first, the doctors said that Loraine would never walk again, but praise God; she is walking and healing up slowly, and doing well considering all that she had been through. Her family, as well as mine, consider me a hero, but I just did what I had to do in a terrible situation and I thank God for sending me an angel in a time of great need. Loraine and I have formed a bond of friendship that will last forever, and we always check on each other. Thank you for letting me share my angel experience with you.

Angel 13/Of Our Overall Health

This image, mostly in cool blues, yellows and greens, shows this angel, head bowed, rendering his healing power onto one, or many, of his children. White healing light radiates from his being, while a blue dove flies overhead, a symbol of God's healing power. If we are able to be open, and have faith, that healing power, that healing light and love, can take place instantaneously.

THE FAMILY THAT PRAYS TOGETHER

Margie

In 1997 between the Christmas and New Years Holidays, I suffered a massive heart attack. However, this sounds somewhat different than what actually took place, although, in the end, the results were the same.

This was at the same time as a major 'flu season' in California, and I thought that it was the flu I was getting. I didn't really feel anything around my chest area as all my symptoms were centered in my back. I was truly having miserable back pain. This was approximately two weeks before the Christmas Holiday.

At this time I was working full time in the Probation Department of the court system, specifically getting reports and files ready for the Juvenile Court Department Office. The files were for the court clerks going into the court.

We have a rather large family, and unfortunately, because of conflicting schedules, we all could not get together on Christmas Eve or even on Christmas day. We decided to get together on the next Saturday between Christmas and New Years, which worked better for everyone.

I worked all day Friday, the day before we were all going to get together, and had a hair appointment Saturday morning. However, during those last two weeks, because of the back pain, I was really slowing down, and after the hair appointment, could hardly get to my home. When I did arrive I instructed my husband and two sons to rush me to the nearest emergency room, as, and the only and best way I can describe it, 'my mind and body functions were leaving me.'

In the ER, the examining doctor said I was having a heart attack; however, I was surprised as there was absolutely no history of heart problems on my side of the family. My doctor said that this heart attack did not come overnight, but that it was in the process of coming for the past several weeks. As I was wheeled into the operating room family members were running along side of me, and I was in a state of shock, confusion and disbelief.

I blanked out, and the next thing I remember, was waking up for a minute or two, and a priest was holding my hand and giving me 'last rites.' I couldn't believe all of this was happening. It was simply beyond comprehension.

Again, I lost consciousness. During this time I had surgery – Angioplasty, where three stents were inserted into my heart. The next day my daughter came to check on me, and it was obvious to her that something had gone wrong. A 'Code Red' was called. I was sent to the MRI unit for photos and it was there that I went into cardiac arrest.

My heart had stopped and the attendants and nurses had to 'paddle' me back, basically from death to life. Then I was sent, once again, into the operating room for more surgery. I was bleeding internally as my heart had been pierced by one of the stents. As unbelievable as it sounds, during this second surgery my heart doctor opened my chest, took out my heart, and was holding it in his hands, checking every possible function, and determined it was beating normally. It seemed as if my heart had actually started to heal itself.

During this time what had taken place was the following: I saw a light, but unlike any light I had ever seen in my life. This light was so extremely bright, brighter then anything I had ever seen, it almost completely overwhelmed me. I wasn't in waking consciousness, as we know it, but in this light I had the most wonderful feeling of my life and was in a state of pure bliss.

In the light I felt I was being lifted. On each side of my body I clearly envisioned three angels holding me up. Six angels were supporting me in every way. I wanted to just stay there; the whole feeling was so wonderful. I was in a complete state of bliss, love and joy; it was this angelic protection I felt had healed my heart.

My sons were outside praying for me to survive, but they intuitively felt that I wanted to go to the other side. However, through the light, the angels and their intense prayers, I was brought back.

After all these experiences I began to really show signs of recovery. Because of the flu season, the hospital was so packed with patients they almost had a difficult time finding a "recovery room" for me. However, one was found. Because my situation was so serious the medical staff began a series of tests to see if my brain had been affected, and, Thank God, all was well. I think I spent a week there before I was released. During this time a neighbor of my mother went to my church and the priest said a private mass for me. And the nurses who attended me said it was a miracle I had survived.

Later at home, and I don't know what the technical term is, but I had been given some photos of my heart. I don't think these were x-rays, but actual photos they are able to take inside the heart. One day my son, Paul, was looking at these photos, and he clearly saw, on one of the prints, a vision of the Blessed Mother.

I am so grateful to the angels, my family and friends for this extended, wonderful gift of life, and most of all, to the beautiful healing white light, who held me in its arms.

In May 2010, I was talking to my youngest daughter about this experience that taken place back in 1997, and she told something I had never known before. She told me she had intensely prayed to angels to take care of me, because she "needed me in her life."

I think most people pray first 'to God,' but she and I were having angelic experiences at the same time without each knowing about the other.

SUNDAY SHAMAN

Angela Taylor

In my twenties, I always had lower back problems. I think this was due to being a typist all day long. One Sunday morning, I woke up and I could hardly walk. This was the worst back problem I have ever encountered. I normally go to chiropractors for an adjustment, but no one was open on Sunday. I felt the need to take some action immediately and not wait until Monday to see if I could get into a chiropractor. I was adamant on not going to an emergency room because I felt that would not help. I then remembered I had a new age newspaper and I frantically shuffled through the pages looking for the healer section. Lo and behold, I found one healer, a shaman, who was open on Sunday. I wasn't sure what a shaman was but since he was in the healer section that was good enough for me. I quickly dialed the number and he was home and could actually see me right away. I asked how much it cost and he said "donation basis." This was incredible because most healers that I had been to charged high fees for the initial visit, and here this man said to pay whatever I could afford.

I had my husband (my first husband at the time), help me get down our apartment stairs and into the car. Deep down, I think a big part of my back problems could have been coming from the stress of intuitively feeling that he had been cheating on me at the time. However, this was something I knew nothing about until years later. We arrived at the shaman's house, which was an ordinary, middle class house. Nothing fancy about it, rather plain, actually. He then explained that there are variations in shamanism in the world, but there are some beliefs that are pertinent to all. For example, communicating with the spirit-world, this consists of animal spirits to bring on the cures. He stated that shamans are able to enter into trancelike states via singing, dancing, meditating, and drumming to enact cures.

He told me to stay fully dressed and helped me onto a "massage like" table. I don't remember any chanting, drumming, or singing taking place. All I know is that he never touched me but waived his hands over my back for about five minutes as I lay there with my eyes closed. Suddenly, a bright, light flashed boldly into my forehead and oozes of peace coursed throughout my body. The shaman asked me, "Did you feel that?" To which I answered, "Yes." He then helped me off the table, and said that the treatment was finished.

And get off the table I did, with NO PROBLEM! I was able to walk without any pain. It was as if a miracle had taken place. I also couldn't believe how fast I could walk. My husband was oblivious to this miracle, probably still wrapped up in his cheating thoughts, but I was ECSTATIC beyond belief. It was incredible! Absolutely incredible!

This angel healing seemed to be the impetus that led to the end of my marriage, make job changes, and today my life is magical.

Angel 8 / Of the World's Children

This is the only image in the Angels of Protection Series in which the protector and the protected can be seen as one. The child angel represents all children, and also represents the protector of all children. Our universe, seen as a sky of stars, along with tangible forms that float in that space, take secondary place to that bright white flash of light, the Omnipresent Protector, behind the angel's head, behind the child's head. And what is that two–toned brown image just under the child's countenance and slightly right of center on the picture plane? A hand reaches up; lifting the child, from the physical world of delusion to a place of ultimate safety, into God's waiting arms.

FLIGHT OF THREE STORIES

Edid Espinal

This event took place in 1971. My mother, Elmis Collado, was getting ready for a trip to her home country, the Dominican Republic. However, we lived in Brooklyn, New York, on Linwood Street. She was to leave the following day.

I was two years old at the time, and was playing in the kitchen, running around, back and forth. I remember playing with the dishes in the sink. I, somehow, got on top of the radiator to reach the sink and play with the dishes. One of my favorite toys was a doll, which I also was playing with, and while playing the doll fell out of the window. Our apartment was three stories up.

I looked out the window to see what happened to my doll, and while looking, the window came crashing down on my back, and flipped me out, causing me to fall the three stories on to the pavement below.

My mother was pre-occupied with packing, but of course, there came a point when she realized she wasn't aware of my presence. She began calling my name and walking around the apartment, looking for me. She then saw that the kitchen window was broken. Apparently the impact of the window falling caused it to break.

I don't know how long this was before she noticed the broken window, but, of course, as soon as she saw it, looked down onto the pavement below, and there I was lying unconscious.

My mother only spoke Spanish, and began screaming for help. She was in a state of complete panic. One of the tenants called the emergency people – the fire department who arrived quickly. They managed to break down the door in the basement, as that was the only way to get to where I was. Let me explain the structure of this apartment complex. It was shaped like a square; i.e., four sides, with a center, in which the tenants could look down, but not go into. The only way to that center area was through a padlocked door.

When the fire department came, my mother was still desperately trying to get to me. They held her back, as they were concerned that I could have internal injuries, and it was necessary not to move me. However, my mother broke away from them, got to me, and scooped me up into the air, into the heavens.

At that point, from an unconscious state, I gasped for air and began to cry. And then the next thing I remember is the hospital, where I was admitted and stayed for about one month for observation. As impossible as it sounds, a child had fallen three stories, had no broken bones and lived to tell about it.

Apparently, my mother, the angel in this story, knew something innately, intuitively, that the EMS people were not aware of. By scooping me up, after being held back as they sincerely felt was the right thing to do, that is, to keep me still, her action ignited my breath once again, and hence, gave me life.

Maybe another way to put it is an angel interfered in a potentially tragic event that had taken place - and saved a child from dying.

ANGEL LIFEGUARD

Rosa Del Toro

I experienced an event in my life in which I believe an angel spoke to me.

We were a normal family doing things routinely like any ordinary family. Both my husband and I had jobs outside the home. However, at home I was responsible for the domestic chores and my husband performed tasks outside the dwelling. I am not going to go into detail listing for you my domestic duties because, if you are woman, you know what I am talking about. However I know some men do understand the complexity of a woman holding a job outside the home and simultaneously being responsible for the domestic chores at home.

The day an angel saved my son's life seems like only yesterday. Time flies. It was in the summer of 2001. I was inside the house and my husband was outside in the back yard. I was sorting laundry, and my husband was cleaning the swimming pool. In order to keep myself entertained I was listening to music on the radio. Quite frankly, I'm surprised I cannot remember my favorite song at the time or my favorite band.

Anyway, while sorting laundry, I heard a voice asking me, "Where is Allen?" Busy sorting laundry and listening to music on the radio, I ignored the voice. I kept working, yet the voice repeatedly told me "Go outside, go outside". I remember suddenly feeling a knot in my stomach. I had no idea why. I remember everything being fine that day.

I remember it was a beautiful sunny summer day. I remember everything going well. I was doing my chores inside and my husband, with our son Allen in the back yard, was doing his chores. I could not understand why I felt a knot in my stomach.

I decided to go outside into the back yard. I asked my husband, "Where is Allen?" He replied that Allen was inside the house. I told my husband that Allen was not inside the house. My immediate thought was to look over to the swimming pool. Looking at the pool, I saw my son floating face down in the water. Upon seeing my son in the pool, I told my husband that Allen was in the pool. Due to being in shock I became immobile. My husband responded by quickly jumping into the pool and retrieved the boy.

My husband proceeded to administer CPR on our son. Fortunately there was no need to call the paramedics because our son regurgitated water from his mouth and started breathing on his own. I believe that angels exist because an angel saved my son's life. The voice I clearly heard, "Go outside, go outside," was an angel's message that ignited the action that saved our son, Allen, from certain death.

On many occasions, I believe, we ignore messages from angels and as a result we pay the price dearly. I thank God that I listened to the prompting of this angel. Our son is alive today.

NIGHT TALKS

Anonymous

My name is Charles, and I am a computer programmer and former gynecologist. This story takes place in my home country, England.

My wife, Jessica, got pregnant at the age of thirty-seven, and therefore was at a high risk of giving birth to a Down's syndrome baby. An amniocentesis was schedule to be performed on her to see if our unborn baby had Down's syndrome, but this dangerous procedure can sometimes provoke a miscarriage.

On the night before the procedure, in a dream, Jessica saw a bright light in the room that looked like a person - an angel was in the room. She felt like she should tell the light about her situation with the upcoming procedure.

In the next coming days, we went on a Healing Pilgrimage to a place called Walsingham. This is the home to the Roman Catholic National Shrine of Our Lady of Walsingham, and the Anglican Shrine of Our Lady of Walsingham. At the pilgrimage, there was a queue (line) of people who needed healing and each one carried a sticker. Each sticker had a number, and people were called in the order of their numbers. There was a paraplegic who, it seemed, needed more healing then we, yet this kindly person donated his place in the queue so that we could get the healing first.

That weekend, Jessica had the exact same angelic experience whereby the angel of light appeared to her, in a dream, and she again spoke to it about her concerns.

In the upcoming week, the results of the amniocentesis showed a normal, male karotype – we would have a baby boy without Down's syndrome.

We felt so blessed and fortunate and realized that angels of protection can come to us from, literally, anywhere. They can be walking toward us on any street of the world's cities or protect a child from the world of the subconscious.

Angel 5/Of My Father

I love my father. He left us in the year 2000. A print of this image hung in his room in the retirement hotel he resided in, until his death, and the story, behind it, follows in my <u>Angel of Protection</u> narrative. The predominant colors – black, white, off-whites, blue and the orangey tans – represent strength and power (black being made up of the three primary colors – yellow, blue and magenta), light of the spirit, the water of life and, lastly the earth and universe. The most powerful color appears in the wings, where it physically serves its highest purpose. The off-whites blast out behind our central figure, as if to ignite the being's consciousness to the brightest 'color' in the image - the full white face of supreme love and protection. The pre-dominate colors

are the orangey tans running through the entire picture. Now look to the upper left – the gift of the universe for all to draw upon, the symbol of life itself - our beloved Father Sun.

A MOTH'S BLESSING

Wil Kinsley

I was in the car with my friend Wesley and we were driving to the Lake Shrine of the Self-Realization Fellowship in Pacific Palisades, California. (If anyplace ever needed an acronym, this is it). Intent on making this a spiritual day for ourselves we were sharing stories of different beliefs and experiences. Wesley grew up in Cypress; one of the stories he told was how the people in that area of the world thought that if you found a big moth in your home, it was the spirit of a loved one, come back to visit or check in on you. Now these aren't the little moths that might eat your clothes, but as he explained they would actually be quite sizable and substantial. I remembered that in my reading I had come across something about this so I just casually accepted it and we moved on to the next subject. That was Wednesday afternoon.

That Saturday night, I was just beginning to start shaving, getting ready to go to work, when out of my left eye I noticed a movement in the hallway outside the bathroom door. I turned my head and there was a huge, 'honkin' moth, fluttering and dancing right outside the door, no more than two feet away from me. Something inside me knew right away what this meant, as my conversation with Wesley came immediately to mind. Instinctively, I knew that this was no ordinary meeting.

In the space of only a few seconds, the silvery moth flew over to me and very lightly landed on the left side of my cheek, where a parent would place a loving kiss upon a child. I was left standing there looking at myself in the mirror with this BIG MOTH... On my face! Now I will tell you this is not normal behaviour for me. I just stared at it and myself, as the wings slowly opened and closed. Other than that, it never moved. Finally, after about twenty seconds, which seemed like a really, long time; I said, "Don't you think I'm taking this awfully well?" After a few more seconds, the moth flew away, straight out the door and I never saw it again.

What I haven't told you is that was the day of my biological father's funeral. We were never close and when I was in the Navy I made a special effort to meet him when I was home on leave for my grandfather's funeral. This ended in anger for me, as I became aware of how much he just couldn't seem to make the effort to get to know his own son, who was even named after him. I went to court and had my name changed to honour my grandfather who had helped to raise me, and that's pretty much where we both left it all those years.

The years did go by though, and I realized that holding on to anger was more of a weight upon me, and learning to let go of it was so freeing for myself and my soul. Perhaps for my father this was a step in that direction to healing the rift between us. But he had one more surprise for me.

About a year later I was able to get an appointment with a well known psychic in Los Angeles, by the name of Brian Hurst. After waiting three months I was very excited about the evening and very much hoping to hear from my mother who had also passed quite recently. There were ten of us in the group and as I waited for Brian to come around to me, you can imagine how I was a little surprised and perhaps disappointed when my father came through. He tried to explain how he was very young when I was born and took it upon himself for our never getting to really know one another. He said that he would be looking out for me, and if I was in need, just call out and he would try to make it happen. Then just as Brian was beginning to turn to someone else, as it seemed another entity was coming through, he said, "Tucker." I was stunned. I asked him to repeat himself. "What did you just say?" Tucker was the name I had changed. Nobody except for my immediate family ever knew my name was Tucker.

This book is about angels and I suppose this is perhaps my way of explaining how angels come in many forms. From the angels we've all heard of in religion or tales, to our personal guides who seem to be assigned to us; and departed family that, much to my surprise, came back into my life. As for how he is doing on that promise of help my father made to me? I moved to Austin and everything is working out great… just great. Thanks, Dad.

DRAMA ON THE SEVENTH FLOOR

Rob Jacobs

My name is Rob Jacobs and I am an artist living in the Los Angeles area. Toward the end of 1999, I asked my father if he would like one of my angel art pieces to hang above his bed in his retirement home. He enthusiastically said, "Yes," and chose what was then known as Angel 5, now called **Angel 5 / Of My Father.** Then, without any pre-conscious thought, I said the following words: "This angel will protect you." I believe this was a spiritually evoked statement because, about six months later, this angelic premonition came to pass, which literally saved my father's life.

When I visited my father, who resided at a retirement hotel in Westwood, California, the ritual was to call him first, which I did without exception. Heading home from my art studio one day, located in the Mid-Wilshire section of Los Angeles, across from the County Museum of Art, the thought "see your father" flashed in my head. It was so strongly pronounced that I immediately turned around and headed for Westwood. The intense thought, "see your father," turned into a voice. I had not called him, but "see your father" kept pounding in my head. My heart was racing by the time I arrived at his room on the seventh floor. I banged on the door, but all I could hear was the blaring of the television. I ran down to the office, got the staff to open his door, and found him lying on the floor, unconscious. It took the paramedics only a few minutes to reach us, and they were able to revive him from insulin shock. Without their help he would have been gone. I knew then, without a doubt, that the angel hanging over his bed had protected him by acting as a messenger to me. He had been plucked from his body's eternal rest. However, a year later he passed on peacefully during the night. He was ninety-three years old, and had lived in every decade of the twentieth century.

My artwork is an organic outgrowth from the remnants of my work as a photo retoucher to the advertising and entertainment industries. Having been a commercial artist for many years, my dream was to do my own images, which I call "fine art." This dream was ignited around 1990 by the great graphic designer, Larry Vigon. Larry had designed album covers for some of the most famous records, cassettes, and CDs, in the history of the recording business, including Eric Clapton, Fleetwood Mac, Chicago, Counting Crows, Carole King, Frank Sinatra and many others. He is also the author and illustrator of the extraordinary book, *DREAM*. Having come over to my studio to view some work I was doing for him, he glanced down at one of the palettes that I create doing artwork. He noticed a unique blending of colors and shapes, emerging from the palette, left over from mixed colors, and the cleaning of brushes and airbrushes. This inspired me to start saving the palettes (9"x12" pieces of tracing paper), which was a mixture of paint, dyes, bleaches, glues, gels and masking fluid, all used in my process of photo retouching. These palettes became the materials that enabled me to begin building my own art. Through Larry's intuition and awareness, I was finally on the path leading me to finding my own voice.

By 1992 I began seriously working, exploring techniques with my palettes. In short, I was creating images, using them in a collage technique. After making my first piece, a surreal and abstract landscape, "Of Sleeping Warriors, Of Spirit Buffalo, Of Phantom Highways," I started seeing images literally jumping out of it. It was populated with impressionistic figures of animals (real and mythic), faces, bodies, imagined creatures, suns, moons, stars, landscapes, planets, ghostly figures.

My technique, in creating the angel images, involved first finding an angel image, from the past, that resonated with me on physical, emotional, mental and spiritual levels. I then made a print of it, and started turning it into my "own angel," through retouching, re-drawing and eliminating, or almost eliminating, the facial features. Eliminating these features, I felt, gave the image a more 'universal feel.' Once the angel was right for my purpose, I then transferred it to clear plastic film and turned to my palettes for the background art. Once I had found the right background and positioned the angel image, the piece was finished. Now I had my original art piece or what I often referred to, from my days as a commercial artist, as "the finished art," from which I could make any kind of print, at any size, scan it for digital purposes, or have it transferred to photographic paper or canvas, which I would have mounted, and then enhance the image with dyes, acrylics or add any other materials that were appropriate.

The spontaneity of the pieces that followed brought about a freedom of design, fluidity of technique, and a subconscious quality. They seem to evoke the universal processes of memory, imagination and the dream state, raw experience pieced together into metaphors of inner life, expanded and transformed by the mysterious logic of the hidden, unconscious self. The viewer discovers new images that emerge from the work every time it's looked at, and I am always discovering hidden images when I begin, and after, the process of assembling it. I work in other disciplines and techniques, the one common theme being the use of my own palettes.

I began creating the angel images, first from an intuitive feeling that I had to make them, and then soon after that, very much in the same mode as the experience with my father, I heard a voice telling me, "make a series of angels." Still, I was not personally aware of the major meaning behind this series. I did, however, feel that any series with angels would be conducive in helping me heal some of my own personal issues. It seemed logical and rational that any positive input could have that effect. When I said to my father "This angel will protect you," I was still not aware of the big picture behind the images. Only after the emotional and powerful experience with him was the meaning behind the series made known and clear to me, resonating with my consciousness. Since that time some of the most joyous moments of my life have been in sharing these images with others.

Angel 14
Of the Earth's Rivers and Oceans

Presiding over the waters – waters that ignite the senses of adventure, romance, love, and fear. Surrender to that being of gold and blue; let go of the fear and you will be protected. Sometimes it's not easy, but fear never works, and courage always does. The boat, symbolic of every one of life's experiences, is sitting under that white moon – God's love and all protecting presence.

THE MAN IN THE WAVES

Laurie Weichman

It had been a warm, sunny, wonderful summer's day and I had taken my three sons, ages seven, five and three to the beach. The ocean was such a beautiful, deep blue and we loved playing in the waves and in the sand. We were all tired but happy by the day's end. The sun was starting to set, and as I began to pack everything up, my oldest son (who wears a prosthetic leg due to a birth defect) asked me, "Mom, I'm all sandy. Can I go rinse off in the water real quick?" I told him, "Okay, but just a rinse off," because we were leaving very soon.

I continued packing and about a minute later I glanced towards the ocean, expecting to see my son all rinsed off and walking towards me. To my utter horror, I didn't see him anywhere at all! I stood on tiptoe scanning the waves and I could not see any human figure whatsoever. In a state of panic and fear my thoughts were: what in the world am I going to do? How will I ever find him? There was absolutely no one around to ask for help. Cell phones weren't invented yet.

My heart started to race, the panic became more intense, and a horrible, frantic feeling welled up inside of me. I stood there frozen for a few seconds trying to think what to do. All of a sudden, I saw two heads way out in the water. As they got closer, I saw that a man was walking out of the ocean carrying my son in his arms! With great relief, I awaited them, and very soon they reached our blanket. The stranger gently set my son down on the sand and I hugged my precious child tightly.

"Oh, my goodness, what happened to you?" I asked my son. He replied, "I went down to the water's edge to wash off, but the waves were farther back from the sand than usual so I had to walk farther out to reach the waves to wash the sand off. Then, out of nowhere, a big wave came and pulled me into the water, farther and farther out, and I couldn't swim back. It wouldn't let me. I couldn't reach the bottom either and the waves kept pulling me under and turned me over and over like summersaults. I couldn't get my head up to breathe and I thought I was going to drown. Then I bumped into this nice, very tall man. He was just <u>standing there,</u> way out in the ocean all by himself. He told me, "Don't worry, son. I've got you." He was so strong. He picked me up in his arms and held me tight. Then he just walked me up to the beach to you."

I turned to grab a towel to cover my son and hold him close to me with great relief. I looked up to thank the man but I didn't see him anywhere. It was as if he had vanished into thin air. I looked quickly to my left and right and down the beach and in the water but he was nowhere in sight. I asked my son, "Where did the nice man go?" He coughed up some water as he replied, "I don't know. He was just here a second ago."

Who was that very tall man who could stand on the bottom of the deep ocean and walk easily through the waves? Where was the man who had saved my son? I had this amazing realization, and told my son, that this man must have been an angel sent by God to save his life! My son's eyes opened wide with awe!

My son is now thirty years old, married and a doctor of clinical psychology. He specializes in adolescents and has already saved children's lives. But we will both remember forever that day on the beach with total gratefulness.

Thank You, Blessed God.

A RIVER OF GRACE

Tom White

I grew up in an area to which many urbanites would blithely label me as "a hick". Red dirt, wheat fields, oil derricks and football made up my world in small town Oklahoma. My dad was in the oil field occupation when I was young so the time that we spent together as a family was rare to say the least. I remember this one time when we went out to the '5 mile hole', otherwise known as "Parker's Bridge." Some farmer had put old cars all along the bank of the river there. His purpose was to stop the river from eroding away his farmland, but it turned out, for us, that the cars were good hiding places for some really big catfish! So, needless to say, my father loved it out there.

There was also a small beach where you could rest and have a campfire nearby. The water wasn't too deep nor was it too strong in current, except maybe to an eight year old, which is what I was at the time. We were out there alone, just mom, dad, younger brother Billy and myself. Billy and I were having fun splashing and swimming while mom and dad seemed to be relaxing out in the deeper water near the base of the bridge. They had their backs turned from us and were looking at something over by the bridge so they didn't notice when their oldest son, me, stepped off into a hole that had been created by the current. I didn't have time to yell or make any noise except the sound that's made when one slips beneath the surface. I remember desperately fighting the current trying to pull myself back to the surface. I made it, but only for a fraction of a second, barely enough time to gasp a breath before I was pulled back down beneath the water. This cycle repeated itself again with me fighting to get back to the light above me, while the current seemed just to want to keep me down there in the hold. I broke the surface one more time but was getting so tired that I was pulled back under again. Those brief moments when I would make it up to the air, I could see my parents standing about ten yards away from me with their backs turned. I could not get their attention.

As I slipped below the last time I thought, "This is it." I was frightened, helpless and alone. It was at this point that a hand reached down from the top of the water and grabbed me by the hair of my head. As the hand pulled me up and out of the water, I glanced up to see this person's face and saw a young, blond-haired man of medium build. He picked me up and carried me to the bank of the river. There he set me on the sand and called my parents over to make sure I was okay. The man smiled, said something about the young boy stepping in a hole too big for himself. He then said it appeared that I was going to be all right and walked off.

Now let me explain something to you so you will understand this as I do. First of all, my family and I were out there totally alone. No other cars were around at all and the nearest farmhouses were miles away. This is a very small town in Oklahoma and my parents were raised in this area and lived there all of their lives. They both said they had never seen this man before, nor, may I add, have any of us ever seen him since. He basically appeared out of the blue, saved me and was gone.

In the years since this incident, I have become a police officer, private detective, news director over several stations as well as an anchorman. I have learned to look upon stories with a certain amount of distance from emotional entanglements that can make 'one thing appear to be another.' I deal with facts and evidence and use them as the foundation for the decisions that I make. Long before television brought us shows like "Highway to Heaven" or "Touched by an Angel" this eight year old boy was both "touched" and "saved" and the facts definitely speak to me of a heavenly influence. What do they say to you?

Angel 4 / In Time of War

In writing about my 'anti-war' piece, Taps is Played for the World, I stated the following: "The impetus that inspired this piece was first, the realization that an innocent child could be born and in later life spend years killing other human beings." I believe that we are all children of God, and wars are waged for a variety of reasons. A religion cannot start a war. Dispossessed, hurt, angry men and women start wars, often using religious scripture as a rationale for their actions. The predominate colors in this image are red, white and blue – colors of the American flag, but, for me, and on a bigger picture, represent all countries and all flags. The other elements in this image are the angel (in shades of black – essentially all of the primary colors – hence all of God's colors) and the rising sun - symbolic of strength, energy, protection, joy and love.

HORROR ON A GASOLINE TANKER

Al Cramer

My name is Albert Joseph Cramer and I am 85 years old now. I grew up in North Hollywood, California, and got drafted into the army at the age of eighteen. They were recruiting for the U.S. Merchant Marine Academy at Kingspoint, New York and I wanted to get in there. I needed recommendations from two very important people in my community and a congressman. My grandfather, luckily was able to secure these for me. He got references from the president of Bank of America and the principal of my high school, plus a congressman he knew. This enabled me to move to New York and I began my studies at Kingspoint.

My first assignment was to be sent to Houston, Texas, to board a gasoline tanker headed for England. This was during World War II. I was known as a "cadet", crew midshipman and was nineteen years old at the time. I had a nice room on the ship and was able to continue my studies towards a college degree. Everything was running smoothly and we were able to unload the one hundred thousand barrels of gasoline on shore, into a giant round tank.

Suddenly we heard the air raid siren and several airplanes started dropping loud, whistling bombs. We ran back to the ship and watched the horror as every other American ship in the harbor, started being blown to bits. It would only take, one tiny spark, to blow up our entire ship because it was filled with gasoline fumes, which we were frantically hosing down.

I was scared but calm at the same time. My fellow shipmates were out of control. Some were bending over crying madly or lying on the floor in anguish. I said a prayer and asked God to forgive me for any bad things I had done in my life. I then decided to watch the bombs drop and thought, along with my fellow shipmates, "this is it."

Suddenly the bombing stopped cold. Every ship in the harbor was destroyed but the ship I was on. We all thought it was an absolute miracle to still be alive! The crew members labeled me "Iron Al" for the calmness that I displayed during the crisis. We were told we could have a week's vacation since our ship could not sail anywhere with the tons of debris in the area. I headed off on a train to Paris and had the time of my life, which was so sorely needed after that harrowing experience. To this day, I will never forget the protection that came to us. It had to be an angel from God!

Angel 3 / Of Intuition

What is intuition? The first definition given in Funk and Wagnall's is "quick perception of truth without conscious attention or reasoning." and, as far as my experience goes, is a perfect definition. When I asked my father if he would like one of my angel images to hang in his room in the retirement hotel he lived in, and he gave me an affirmative answer, without any conscious thought, and immediately, I said the following words, "This angel will protect you." As it turned out, those intuitive words that I spoke turned out to be absolutely true. This experience with my father is related in this book. This image, with the

angel rendered in shades of neutral grey stands, almost in profile, while in the background life of the universe is taking place, represented by abstract and recognizable shapes in yellows, oranges, blues, browns, and a mixture of these colors. But what is the brightest color in the image? It is the huge flash of white light behind the figure's head – the light of perception, love and intuition.

LIFE COACH

Isaac Evans

I was at my wits end in 2005 after resigning from a principal/teacher position. The 2004-2005 school year was tremendously difficult and disappointing. I had accepted a position that was completely over-taxing on my skills and abilities.

A year earlier, I had been approached by the school board chairman of a private school. I had been teaching third and forth grade in an elementary school, and had successfully taught there for five years. The chairman asked me if I would consider being a principal of their K through Tenth grade school. Because I knew most of the students and teachers from church activities and school functions, I believed that accepting the position was a call from God. However, little did I know that the position required at least two or three people to successfully fulfill the requirements of this job. The salary was less than a teaching position in a regular district. Being a principal of a school is a full-time duty and required most of my attention. Along with that responsibility, I taught six classes. Being a teacher requires full-time preparation for lesson planning, class instruction, and other school activities. To make a long story short, I experienced a difficult year with both teaching and administrative duties. On top of that, my wife and children saw very little of me during the week and on weekends. I was mentally, physically, socially and spiritually drained. I was broken. I was disappointed and believed that I took on too much. I was very frustrated. I looked to God for answers, but I couldn't hear Him. I felt that I had been left to be defeated and, and I was overwhelmed. What was most painful was that I looked to the staff for help, and they offered little to none. There was so much anger that I was holding inside. Let's just say, I was saving face. I didn't want to unload my discouragement on my family. I love my wife and children dearly. My children were so young, but they could see straight through to my heart that I was devastated. They knew that their dad was not happy. I needed someone to help me get out all of the issues I had flustering in my brain. I cried out to God, but it just didn't seem like He heard me at the time.

I went to Los Angeles to the musician's union to take care of some business for a project I had started in 2001. While there, I picked up a spiritual magazine that had many spiritual mind coaches and spiritual leaders. I took the magazine with me. While at home, I read each one of the advertisements. There was one life coach that I was immediately impressed with - her testimony. Her story of depression and how she kicked it in the butt really made me identify with her. Her name was Michelle. I emailed her, and told her exactly what I have been sharing in this story. I also asked her for help. It was around a day later that I received her response to my email. She set up a phone conference a couple days later, and set up life coaching sessions to deal with the anger and depression I was experiencing. These sessions that I had with my life coach proved to be better than all of the schooling and training I had previously gone to school for. She helped me to identify the blocks in my thinking that were keeping me from achieving and truly experiencing my dreams and goals. She assisted me in positive thinking exercises and affirmations. She challenged me with a variety of take home assignments, to monitor my thinking patterns. The exercises helped me to release negative thought patterns and adopt new and positive thought patterns. If I had any questions or concerns while doing my assignments, I could always call her. Even now, I email her or share my success stories with her. She responds to me even with her busy schedule. Because of Michelle's unselfish service in helping me identify methods of mind management, I have been able to think more clearly and positively. I have been able to attract much more positive results in my life. I was able to complete my musical project of the Isaac Evans' **My Journey** CD on July 2008. I also have completed eleven years of successful teaching experience. I am happily married for fifteen years now. I have two fabulous children. Of course I have had difficult situations come up in my life since working with Michelle, but I am able to see each experience as a stepping stone in being the unique and wonderful person that God created me to be. I consider Michelle an Angel of Protection, because she helps me and thousands of people continually work through depression and feelings of defeat. I am so glad that she takes the time to assist me in so many areas of life. She makes herself available, internationally, to help people work through issues, and does this in a beautifully holistic way. I am amazed at her excellence in the work she does. I am so much better because of her help, and it goes to prove what I have thought for many years: angels do not need wings to lift us up into God's beautiful protective white light.

A DAUGHTER'S GIFT

Les Gerber

As I sit before the computer screen and try to find the right keys to tell this strange tale, I am amazed that I am able to even think about the past month. This is a story that may seem to the reader to come out of the deepest depths of the imagination. For I am writing this after having been on the brink of death, and was saved by good luck or a daughter's instinct –most likely a protecting angel.

The story begins on September 14th, 2006. While waiting for my daughter-in-law, JoAn, to arrive for the chores she does for me each Thursday, I was attacked by severe chills and unstoppable shaking. By the time Jo arrived I was wrapped in a heavy blanket, which did nothing to abate the attack. Jo was worried when she asked me what was wrong. I could not give her an answer for I didn't have one. After about twenty minutes the chills left, and the shaking stopped.

The evening went on as normal. I prepared dinner, ate it, and then settled in to watch the evening television shows.

Friday was the usual. This was the day I did my weekly grocery shopping, and by nine in the morning I was on my way to the store. The experience of the night before was a thing of the past. The day went by like almost every other day.

About eight that evening I was sitting in my chair musing about various topics as I watched television. Suddenly, I began to shake as I had the evening before, and began to have severe chills again. I again wrapped myself in a heavy blanket, which did no good. After about the same length of time as the day before, the attack dissipated. Although I began to take this attack more seriously, I did not even begin to think about seeing a doctor, let alone go to the urgent care facility.

Saturday came and went. There were no further incidents, not even in the evening.

I went into bed about nine that evening, turned on the television and proceeded to fall into a deep sleep. This was not unusual, for over the years I have found that the tube is a great sleep inducer.

I was awakened with severe chills and uncontrollable shaking. I wrapped the blanket around myself to no avail. I do not know how long it lasted, but when it was over the clock read two thirty. Before rolling over to return to sleep, I told myself that this was not a passing matter, and that I had to see a doctor in the morning.

Sunday morning came and I did not go through my usual routine. I called the urgent care unit of my medical group and was told that they did not open until eight in the morning. I left the house about seven forty five and drove to the urgent care unit.

Before leaving I thought about calling my son Dan to advise him of what I was doing. I decided that I did not want to disturb him and his family on a Sunday morning for something that may amount to nothing. I arrived at the urgent care unit, paid my fee and waited to see a doctor.

The nurse who took my blood pressure and temperature asked me what was wrong. When I told her she seemed stunned. My pressure and temperature were fine. I was shocked when she told me how low the blood pressure was, since I do tend to high blood pressure. I told her that given the trauma I had been through I was pleasantly surprised.

When I talked to the doctor he seemed confused. He ordered x-rays, and checked all of the vitals. The one factor that seemed to point the process in a specific direction is when I told him that I was unable to give him a urine sample. He asked if I was able to at least pass a few drops. I tried to no avail.

Before I knew it a catheter was being inserted. Once in, my bladder was drained, and a bag was attached to my left leg. The urine was analyzed and showed that there was an infection in the bladder.

I was sent home with the catheter and told to make an appointment with my urologist.

The week passed as I tolerated the usual annoyance of a catheter. In fact, I attended the Rosh Hashanah services on Saturday.

Sunday came and I did my usual. In the early afternoon I sat down before the computer to try to write. Before I got to the writing the doorbell rang. I went to the front door and could see a bouquet of flowers covering the face of whoever was delivering them. I opened the door. The bouquet came down. The face before me was my daughter Diana.

I was shocked. She told me that she felt the need to see me since we spoke on the phone on Thursday. She said that she did not like how I sounded. Did I sound sick? I was not at my brightest because of the prostate situation, but I did not believe I sounded that bad.

Whatever reason brought her it was great having her with me. She said that she planned to return to Washington the following Thursday, September 28.

On Tuesday, Diana accompanied me to the urologist's office, where I had the catheter removed. The doctor examined me and said that the prostate was back to normal size.

I left the doctor's office with Diana feeling like I was just released from a heavy burden.

The next two days Diana and I visited and talked about everything. On Thursday I went to bed at my usual time. I turned the television on and promptly fell into a deep sleep.

I awoke later in the night with a pain in my chest and up into my neck and right ear. It felt as if a truck were sitting on my chest. There was nothing sharp, only heaviness. I went to the bathroom to urinate, and when I returned to my bed the pain became unbearable. I screamed for Diana as I sat on the bed and held my upper chest to try to abate the pain. She came, and I told her to get the medics. She called 911 and spoke with the operator as I writhed in pain.

Although the medics were there in a matter of minutes, to me it seemed like an eternity. They entered the bedroom and tried to mitigate the pain. They said the ambulance would be along in a few minutes. I of course did not realize that the first to arrive were the fire department paramedics. The ambulance was along in a matter of minutes. I was placed on a gurney and taken to the ambulance. I remember asking Diana to follow us in the car. She said that she was going to ride in the ambulance.

Once in the ambulance I thought we would be off in seconds. Instead they began hooking me up to a device, which I believe communicated my condition to the hospital. By this time the nitroglycerine they gave me before taking me to the ambulance began to abate the pain. We finally took off and rode down the streets at a leisurely pace. Only the red lights were blinking. However, we arrived at the hospital in a matter of minutes.

It was then that I realized that the time was four thirty in the morning. I apparently got the attack sometime around four.

Once inside, I was sedated by the hospital staff. A doctor on duty gave me a preliminary examination, which apparently showed nothing. A second run-through showed that I had a heart attack. I lay in the emergency room until about one in the afternoon when the cardiologist accompanied me to the operating room where he inserted a stint in the artery to the heart. I was greatly surprised when I asked him if I were to be sedated or at least numbed, and he said no. I felt a pin prick and that was all.

I learned, after the procedure, that I had severe blockage of the artery, and that the severity of the attack generally felled at least 50% of the people who suffer such an attack.

Through it all my children Dan and Diana stayed with me. Although there was not much to say, knowing they and their families were with me was support that helped me keep a positive attitude.

My recovery is now in progress. As you the reader can surely tell I am making headway, by just the fact that I am writing this just one month after the attack.

However, the more interesting part of the story is that my daughter was with me when I had the attack. What made her believe that something was wrong? Why did the attack occur on the day that she was to return home? Life has many strange and unexplainable occurrences.

I am very much aware of the fact that if she were not there at the time, I would not be here to relate this life adventure to you the reader.

Angel 2 / Of the Earth's Animals

Rising up over the mountain he stands in a field of ochre, surrounded by animals, many in shades of warm grey - some recognizable, some not. All are protected, including those not represented in this image, some of our closest friends – cats and dogs. The source of physical life, the sun, appears high above the angel's right shoulder. The two abstract red shapes (top right of image) radiate the loving energy necessary for the protection of the trillions of God's creatures, who were put here to teach us many lessons necessary for our own survival, and most importantly, the lesson of unconditional love.

RED SKYE IN THE MORNING

Marilyn Dalrymple

I believe most of the angels in my life have been in the form of animals. The pets I've brought into my life and home always seem to appear during times when my heart is broken, my spirit non-existent or my health is in jeopardy.

One of my most memorable pets lived with me during a time of great stress and upheaval. I was alone raising three adolescents. My three children, in their rebellion, tried everything adolescents could do to push the boundaries, and break a parent. I was exhausted, scared, lonely, and my hair was turning white due to worry.

"Skye," waltzed into my life in June of 1990. He was a thirty-pound puppy with paws as big as coffee mugs. His American Kennel Club papers identified him as "Red Skye in the Morning." "Skye" was spelled with an "e" ending because, from the moment I saw him, I knew he was extraordinary.

I chose his official name partly because the distinctive Alaskan malamute's markings on his cream-colored coat were splashes of burnished copper. But the name also tied him to his Antelope Valley home, a place of arid and stark stretches of sand set afire mornings and evenings with pyrotechnic-like red sunrises and sunsets. While a puppy, the fur on Skye's head shot up into a modified Mohawk and his lip's pink leather seemed to curve into a perpetual grin. Curious, mischievous and most of all playful, he'd glide on his snowshoe-like-paws across a slick floor, enjoying the ride, then scramble, scamper and tumble trying to prevent the obvious meeting with the wall he was about to encounter. During his first autumn, and when the leaves fell from our fruitless mulberry trees, the rambunctious pup performed pirouettes, trying to catch each leaf before it hit the ground.

I'd confront him with my hand on hips, in the backyard. He'd be wearing a 'who me' expression on his face covered with fresh dirt, and his front paws inches deep in another hole. But, soon my clown-pup matured into a wise and noble dog. During quiet times, he'd lie by the bookshelves, front paws crossed, head held high, seemingly lost in thought. I could only wonder what secrets of life he was contemplating.

He exhibited strength, wisdom and calmness and through his steady gaze, he transferred these qualities to me. Like ballroom dancers floating across a polished floor, we did not need words to communicate. Our conversations consisted of nudges, gentle tugs and the stroking of his fur. He'd rest a paw on my arm or his muzzle on my knee, while exchanging glances. His thoughtful gold-colored eyes were a language unto themselves.

While I'd work, Skye would curl his huge body into a ball and lay under my desk, barely leaving room for my feet. I'd have to take giant steps over him while he slept, stretched end-to-end, in front of the couch. The places where my large companion rested and slept are now so obviously empty. Passing through the stages of his life much too fast, and before I was ready, my best friend died. *I'll never get over missing him,* I thought. What do I do now? How do I fill the void?

As time passed I sensed my mourning would only hinder his journey from his earth-bound frame to his becoming a brilliant spirit. *I know what he would want,* I had thought. I found a local animal rescue and volunteered to work with pets that were not as fortunate to be part of a family.

Soon after Skye's death and while driving to the pet rescue sanctuary where I was volunteering, I spotted a large cream and copper-colored animal standing by the road's side. My heart skipped several beats while I stared at the animal that stood stone still. He was looking straight into my eyes. The world disappeared for a brief moment, or was it for an hour? Pulling off the road, I looked back, goose bumps rising on my arms. The animal was gone, but how? Where? Open fields surrounded me, and the large animal had just disappeared. Leaving my car, I combed the prickling spikes of yellow grasses that stood soldier straight in the parched earth, but the animal was nowhere to be found. Had I imagined it? NO! I'd seen an animal that looked exactly like Skye.

Or was it Skye in a new form? I've heard that spirits of those who were greatly loved return to us just before leaving the earth plane and entering to the next realm, so those left behind would know that all is well. *I KNOW I HAD SEEN MY BELOVED PET, AND NO ONE WILL CONVICE ME OTHER WISE.* And I knew if anyone deserved to be an angel – a messenger of hope – it was Skye.

Falling leaves, caring for homeless pets, but most of all the red skies in the morning, all reminders of a much-missed companion. All reminders that each of us must celebrate, not mourn, the dance of life and death.

GYPSY WITH AN ATTITUDE

Marilyn Dalrymple

Gypsy was a tiny, flea ridden, sorry sight when I first spotted him in a playpen at a pet store. He was the one remaining kitten from an unexpected litter. It seemed no one wanted the white and gray kitten, but I could tell at a glance, he was just the kind of little character I liked. He looked mischievous, curious and intelligent. How could other animal lovers not have seen all these qualities in him?

I took him home with me and within two weeks Gypsy made it clear to our Alaskan malamute and English Springer spaniel that he was in charge. He quickly taught me that dry cat food was beneath him and only certain types of canned food would fulfill his dining requirements. Snubbing the beautiful wicker basket, which was lined with a pillow and blue and pink plaid baby blanket, he chose to nap on the queen-sized bed in our guest room. His favorite spot was in the center of the sun-splashed, down-filled comforter.

I could only pet Gypsy on his terms. He definitely had an attitude and a time schedule. No petting before 4:00 p.m. Between 8 and 10pm he had better be petted, or loud, demanding "meows" would fill the entire house. Absolutely no baths at any time, and combing or brushing sessions were to last no longer than 2 minutes, 'tops."

His routines went like clockwork and he seemed to thoroughly enjoy the station he held at our home.

Then his schedule was thrown off. I had been diagnosed with cancer. Doctor appointments, two surgeries and chemotherapy treatments kept me away from him much of the time and caused chaos with his schedule. It took several months before things became normal at home and my healing process began.

Gypsy seemed to size up the situation and put a plan into action. He'd lie on the couch or in bed and would jump up on me, landing light-as-a-feather on my chest. He'd curl up, purring like his body had the engine of a Harley Davidson. The warmth and vibrations from this rascally friend was more comforting than any medical therapy could possibly provide.

As I healed, Gypsy visits became less frequent and slowly he retreated back to his bed in the guest room and his regular routine. He seemed to sense that things were slowly getting back to normal.

As much as I appreciated all that the doctors and medical community had done for me, I have a special place in my heart for my little in-house healer. I will never understand how Gypsy had the wisdom to know all was not well with me, just like I can't understand how he sensed my healing was complete. I am beginning to think, however, that it is not the sun shining through the windows that causes the warmth and light on the guest room bed, but that it emanates from the 'angel with an attitude' that sleeps there.

Angel 11 / Of Money and Finance

In the physical world, not the spiritual or metaphysical, everything revolves around money and finance. In objectively standing back one can see this is true. We paid for the bed we sleep in, the clothes we put on, the breakfast we are eating, the car and gas it takes to get to work, lunch during the day, school for the kids, and then, back home to eat and watch programs that have money themes on our TV set.

Running into problems with money is part of everyday life, especially as life becomes more difficult within areas we cannot foresee – recession, depression, job loss, health issues, other emergency situations, and it goes on indefinitely. These huge issues placed Angel 11 /

Of Money and Finance ***on the cover of our book.***

The abstracted, somewhat disturbing eagle image, in the top left part of the picture plane, could go on any currency. And the blue sun in the image, above our angel's head, represents love, light, bliss, joy and protection.

DOLLARS FROM HEAVEN

Edid Espinal

On a Wednesday, in 2010, I was intending to call my mother who lives in Massachusetts. I mistakenly called my sister, Jolie, instead.

My sister was very happy to hear from me. In our conversation, she relayed that she was having some difficulties, among them, finding work and generally going through a lot of emotional stress. During the conversation I was trying to motivate her with some affirmations, for example, to "Not give up," and I was attempting to give her some information from my own spiritual path of meditation, and the power of prayer.

We continued to talk. Since she didn't presently have work she relayed that she was down financially. She asked me to call her ex-husband to see if he would help her in this area. The reason she didn't want to contact him is that, she felt, he was somewhat burnt out on her previous requests for financial aid, which he had contributed to.

I felt intuitively that this wasn't the right thing to do. We kept on communicating and much of this conversation centered in the metaphysical areas and the spiritual world. We have had many conversations of a spiritual nature in the past. I picked up a box, which I had attained from my temple, which was a 'horn of plenty,' a way of saving small amounts of money that could be contributed to the church. On the box are wonderful, positive affirmations for life success, which I wanted to share with her.

I was reading some of these affirmations, and in the middle of this, her phone cut off. The battery was dead. Obviously, I couldn't call back then, so just went on with my normal day.

However, during the conversation, I had relayed to Jolie that I was going to send her some money, and would call her when I sent it so that she would know approximately when to expect it.

I decided to go to the bank, so that I could withdraw the funds that I was going to send her. For some reason, I didn't quite make it to the bank that day, as time got too late.

The next day, Thursday, I went to my temple - my spiritual path, to meditate, maybe pick up some reading material for my sister and myself; the focus was on how I could be of service to her, and to give thanks for the blessings in my life. I had intended to get the funds that day for Jolie. However, since I commuted on public transportation, or by walking, once again, time got away, and I didn't make it to the bank.

On Friday, after dropping my son, Ziggy, off at pre-school, I was running toward home, which I usually do for exercise. During my run, I was thinking different thoughts, some spiritual, others more of the earth, what I was going to do for the day, and also getting the funds for my sister. However, after checking, I did not have my wallet with me. Since I had to go home first to get it, I decided I would stay to take care of a massage client, who was coming that afternoon, and, generally, get things together, before heading out to run some errands, including my visit to the bank. I initially had planned on sending Jolie around twenty dollars, as things had been rather tight for us and about all I could send her, but, with the massage client that afternoon, I would be able to send her more money.

As I was running what appeared to be a piece of paper was floating in the air near me. The day was windy, and this piece of paper almost smacked me in the face. And then it started to drop to the pavement. As I looked down I could see it was a twenty-dollar bill. I stepped on it, so that it wouldn't fly away, and as I reached down to pick it up, there was another twenty-dollar bill. I had no idea where these bills came from. They were just there! As I was about to pick up the second twenty, I looked slightly up, and there was another twenty dollar bill, but I could see that this was in a small roll of twenties – a total of three more, which added up to one hundred dollars. I was in a state of excitement, and began looking all over for the origin of these funds. There was not a soul around. Not one person, anywhere!

I picked up the money, and I started running back home. I was so excited, and in a state of giddiness. I had done everything I could to find the owner of the funds, but, as I said, there was not one person around and I began thinking: "This is a gift from my sister Jolie's angels to her at a time of need."

As I jogged home all I could think of was how this gift would help my sister, and I was just filled with feelings of love and gratitude.

Ziggy and I had previously bought a card for Jolie, and I put two small prayer books that I had picked up, while in the temple on Thursday, along with fifty dollars from the hundred that I had found, into the mail to her.

I sent the other fifty dollars to another friend, but that is a story for a different time.

TIGER IN THE NEIGHBORHOOD

Anonymous

When my husband Ray and I lived in West Los Angeles during the 1960s we were having trouble with the neighbor across the street. He was an angry alcoholic who took out his feelings in violent ways; one of those ways was by beating up on his wife.

Anyway, we really wanted to move out but we knew we couldn't. We didn't have the money for a new house. However, a strong intuitive feeling told me to check the newspaper. I went to the house ads and there was an ad, "For sale or Trade". I had never seen an ad like that, but I called.

The realtor I talked to became a good friend, helped us get into what we called our Weddington house, loaned us money, paid our closing costs, and was there for us from then on. Tiger Palmer was his name. He was our knight in shining armor.

He also helped us out of a tax jam once. I went to him because we owed $5000 to the IRS, and I couldn't get it from my dad or Ray's father. The IRS had pulled our money out of our accounts at the bank. It was awful. I called Tiger and went in to see him. I told him about it and all he said was, "How much should I make out the check for?" He was truly sent by our angels.

MY PURSE RUNNETH OVER

Anonymous

This all took place around 1980, in San Diego County. On Friday.

I was flat broke and my phone was to be shut off that night unless I could come up with one hundred dollars. It had to be paid by 5pm. There was just no way to come up with the cash. I had zero credit cards, nothing to sell, and no one to borrow the money from. Somehow I had forgotten to pay this bill and I had absolutely no emergency money. I was pretty much living hand to mouth at the time with a two-bit job and apartment to boot.

I needed that phone to be kept on. I absolutely hated living so tightly. However, that day I basically resigned myself to the idea of having the phone shut off. I figured I'd have to have it shut down for a month or two until I could save up some money. This was thirty years ago, before cell phones so, in order to make a call, I would have to go to a public phone booth.

That same day my purse strap broke to bits; let's say this wasn't one of the best days of my life. I needed a new purse, however, since there was no way to buy a new one, and yet, I had to have a purse; the only way to get one was to go to the local thrift store, drop a dollar or two, and get the cheapest one available.

That is exactly what I did. I picked out the cheapest purse and bought it. It was nothing to write home about, just a brown 'saggy baggy' to hold all my items.

When I got home I started undoing the various zippers to put my belongings inside, and lo and behold, to my utter amazement, inside one of the pockets there was a ....

Have I got your attention? The suspense is building! There was a… inside one of the pockets… a….

HUNDRED DOLLAR BILL!

I gasped with delight and said a MAJOR "THANK YOU!"

Somehow, a luminous being, an angel, had interfered in the world of karmic events, and had protected me from a further descent into the financial hole I was living in.

I kept on intoning, "Thank You, Thank You," went down and paid my bill just before the phone was to be shut off.

Now, receiving a gift of one hundred dollars is not going to automatically change one's financial status; however, the wonderful, positive angelic energy of that day began a series of events that elevated my life into the higher realms of the spirit.

Angel 15 / In the Western Deserts

The desert is a place of beauty, home to plants that need no water, mountains so beautiful they touch our souls at the highest chakras, and multitudes of creatures of every variety. It can also be a place of danger and unexpected violence. The angel in this image shows us this big picture – the dark sky of danger (death) and the sky of dawn (life). The yellow sun - a symbol of birth, creation and enlightenment, is reflected on his shoulder as he stands in front of the majestic orange

mountain, and the eagle – a symbol of spiritual protection, brings strength, courage and wisdom. A saying from the Sioux – "Wakan Tanka nici un" – "May the Great Spirit walk always by your side." And that is the Angel of Protection in the Western Deserts.

RESCUE IN DEATH VALLEY

Frank Buddenbrock

Each spring, the Southern California Land Rover Club holds its annual Rover Rendezvous – a get-together of up to one hundred Land Rovers from four clubs: Southern California Land Rover, Land Rover Club of Las Vegas, San Diego Land Rover and Northern California Land Rover.

The Rover Rendezvous is an organized event where Land Rover owners join together for a weekend of off-highway driving and exploring. During the weekend, trip leaders guide drivers through parts of Death Valley. I planned to lead my group to Cerro Gordo, a "ghost town" high in the Inyo Mountains.

To be ready for early Saturday morning departures, many of us get situated and set up camp on Friday evening. After setting up my camp, I made my way over to the check-in to confirm that I would be leading Saturday's Cerro Gordo trip. At check-in I was told that unfortunately the Inyo Crest Mountains and the road to Cerro Gordo were still under several feet of impassable snow. I was truly disappointed that we could not visit Cerro Gordo, and thought that perhaps my group could just tag along on another previously scheduled run. I would wait until the next morning and see if that would be okay with my group.

Saturday morning I recounted the bad news about Cerro Gordo being snowed in, and proposed that we tag along on another run. Unanimously, my group all said they would rather do our own run and not follow another group. Knowing that no other groups were heading out to The Racetrack, I proposed that we go there. To my surprise and delight, no one in my group had been there before. Well, I said, "Let's go."

The Racetrack is a magical place in Death Valley- a dry lakebed, or playa, where rocks move and leave long tell-tale tracks behind them. Why the rocks move remains a mystery, and it is these moving rocks that give The Racetrack its name.

To get to The Racetrack from Panamint Springs, we first traveled west on Highway 190 to Saline Valley Road where we turned north and headed to Hunter Mountain. Coming down from Hunter Mountain through the pinyon pines and Utah junipers, we were soon on Hidden Valley Road. I had just passed a turn-off to the Calmet Mine when I decided that since we had been driving for about an hour and a half, it would be a good place to stretch our legs, get some fresh air, and do a little exploration of the mine. I stopped my truck, and over my FRS hand -held radio told everybody to back up about a hundred feet so that we could make the turn down to the mine.

Everyone backed up and shortly we were headed down the road to the mine. The road continues down the canyon to other mines, but we turned off at Calmet Mine, about a quarter mile down from the main road. For twenty minutes we checked out the mine, took some photos, and drank some water. I began to round everybody up to continue our trip and as we made our way back to our trucks we were suddenly taken aback by an unexpected sight.

Trudging up the steep dirt road came an elderly couple dragging their suitcases behind them. In her hand the woman held a golf club with a white T-shirt tied to it- a signal flag for help. We ran over to the couple to help them, and to find out what had happened.

George and Gail, the elderly couple in their late 70s, had decided the previous day to do a little exploring on their way home from Scotty's Castle. They had traveled a little further down the canyon to another mine and had pulled off the main road to make room for any passing traffic. Unfortunately, George, in his attempt to be considerate of potential passers-by, pulled off a little too far and ended up getting his two-wheel drive Ford Explorer stuck in the soft sand on the road's shoulder. After innumerable unsuccessful attempts to get their vehicle unstuck, George and Gail were forced to spend the night in their truck. Unsure they were going to survive in the desert, Gail's anxiety caused her to be physically sick. Not prepared for a night in the desert, they huddled together to stay warm whispering a prayer for an angel to come save them.

The next morning they waited as long as they could, hoping to be rescued and realizing that there might never be someone coming down the canyon, they decided they would have to walk out to safety. The nearest main road was approximately fifteen miles away, quite a distance to walk in Death Valley during the middle of the day, dragging a heavy suitcase along a rock-strewn dirt road, and, on top of that, these people were almost eighty years old. I can only imagine their joy, and the relief they must have felt to see us.

After George and Gail recounted their unfortunate predicament, we put them and their suitcases into a couple of Land Rovers and drove down the canyon to see if we could extract their truck from the soft sand. I tried a few times to just drive the truck out of the sand, but indeed it was stuck. After attaching a recovery strap to the front of the Explorer and the other end to one of our Land Rovers, we pulled the truck back onto the hard packed dirt road. Followed by our rescuing Land Rovers, I drove George's truck back up the canyon to join the rest of our waiting group.

Now comforted, knowing they had been saved (by an angel), George began to return their suitcases to his truck. I got out of the drivers seat of his truck to make my way around the front to the rear passenger door to help George with his gear. As he moved to place the gun he had been carrying holstered on his hip onto the back seat of his truck, it went off, firing a bullet through the passenger seat and lodging in the driver's door right passed where I had been sitting just ten seconds earlier. Apparently an angel was looking out for me that day, too.

It dawned on me later that we had not planned to go on this run, nor had we planned to head down to the mine where we eventually encountered George and Gail. Indeed, it seems that their prayers had been answered.

George and Gail followed our group out to the main road where we bade our good-byes and wished them well as they disappeared in a cloud of Death Valley dust.

Angel 7 / Of the World's Mothers

This image, rendered in warm colors of the palette – grays, browns, oranges, ochre, sienna, represent the colors of a mother's love – the colors of a sunset. Her right hand is raised in an attitude of blessings, the blessings of the protective mother. Her wings look like a protective shelter, and isn't that what a mother provides - love and protection. I know my beloved mother did before she was taken from us when I was nineteen years old. God, in the philosophy of the east, is often referred to as "Divine Mother." The Lakota call this physical world, "Mother Earth," and they treat it with all the respect due a loving mother.

TWICE AT DAWN

Alison Robinson and Kevin Cramer
Introduction by Angela Taylor

First, I would like to give you some background on my mother, Mavis Cramer, who died at the age of eighty from cancer. I will then go into the angel experiences my brother and sister had on the same day, at the same time, in their respective homes, and how their angelic experiences saved the entire family from intense grief.

My mother was born, Mavis Ida Richert, on February 21, 1925. Little is known about her mother and father as she was adopted by a family in Minnesota when she was a baby. Mavis grew up on a farm. She never spoke much about her farm days because she was a city girl at heart. In Minnesota she became an expert ice skater, high school homecoming queen, USO Queen dancer and proficient secretary. She won the Jitterbug dance queen award in her town. She was a total extrovert and would talk to anyone about anything. Mavis had dark hair, brown, kind eyes and barely reached 5 feet.

She was ecstatic when her adopted parents moved to the Hollywood, California area. There she landed the job as a secretary to the president of a brassiere company.

It was there at the bra factory that my dad, calm and quiet Al Cramer got his first civilian job. He had been in the Navy for ten years and had traveled the entire world. Now it was time for him to settle down. My mom noticed him immediately at work and asked to be introduced right away. Within six months of the introduction they were married.

My mom worked at home as a typist while raising the twins, an older girl sibling and last born son. When the kids were in high school, Mavis got a full time bank office job and stayed there until retirement. Her husband worked for the state of California as a highway engineer. In the last part of their lives, they enjoyed taking cruises everywhere.

She loved to be the center of attention and since her husband was the quiet type, this match seemed to work. Everyone in town knew who she was. She loved to wear fancy clothes and makeup, go to parties, shop in malls, read mystery stories outside by the pool in the sunshine, eat Sees candy and get her hair done. She was a good Catholic and went to church every Sunday of her life. She loved Jeopardy and watched it for forty years. On one of her church, senior bus trips to Nevada, she met the daughter of the Jeopardy host who gave her an autographed picture of him. How she treasured that photograph.

Mavis was always cheerful and active. She would walk the

neighborhood in the early evening with her friend, Kathleen, plus swim in the pool every summer day she could. We thought she would live to be about a hundred years old. She rarely had a sick day in her life. Even when she was sick, she would never miss a day of work. So it came as shock to all of us when she got cancer at age eighty. She had bits of cancer here and there but it originated in her breast. Chemotherapy cured the cancer entirely within about six months and no operation was needed. We thought she could live through anything, so when she got cancer the second time, we all assumed she would pull through it again, just like she did the first time.

Mavis had a live-in caregiver who didn't drive. This meant that the two closest siblings, Alison (one of the twins), and Kevin, would be driving her to doctor's appointments, pharmacies, physical therapy, grocery, etc. They also dealt with Mavis's personality change as most people would have going through the difficult issues of cancer. Mavis seemed to have intense moments of fear, anger, complaining, anguish and despair.

Kevin and Alison heard it all. It was a heavy load for them, emotionally, plus they both worked full time jobs as well. They were glad to help her but it was extremely hard. This is why I think Kevin and Alison were given the angel experiences they had on the day of my mother's death.

Alison's Angel Experience

On December 9, 2005, I suddenly woke up at 4am and felt completely energized and a feeling of relief wafted over me. I didn't have a care in the world! I normally struggle with horrendous back pain in the morning, but the pain was completely gone. I felt so free and uplifted, as if a blanket of goodness and all that is good in the world was all over me. I never felt this way before. It was if something or someone was bathing me in complete and loving energy. It was so very real and the thought had come to me that it could be my mother or an angelic presence that was thanking me for all the hard work and care I had given my mother. It was as if this force field or presence was telling me not to worry about anything, anymore and that all is fine with my mother and she appreciated everything that I had done for her. Normally, when I get up in the morning I race over to my mother's house, barely eating and attending to matters in my own household. But today, I felt that the presence wanted me to take my time and not even turn on my cell phone for any emergency calls. So I followed the feeling of bliss.

Two hours later, my brother, Kevin, called from my mother's bedside and said to come over quickly that she was breathing heavily. I asked, "Do you think this is it?" He said, "Yes." Normally, I would have been absolutely frantic and out of my head to hear this, speeding in my car to get to her bedside. I still felt blissfully relaxed, took my time and ate a snack, packed my vitamins and drove calmly over because I knew that this is what my mother would have wanted. When I got to the house, she had just passed away.

Kevin and I exchanged words and I almost jumped out of my skin when he told me that he suddenly woke up at 4am and relayed to me an experience he had that sounded just like mine. We exchanged stories and his is told below here. We agreed that if we ever had any doubt of the reservation of the separation of the body and the spirit, that this notion had disappeared. We felt that death was a very good thing and something we should never fear. We felt blessed to have had the experiences we did and as we shared them with the family members, they too felt healed from any type of intense grief.

Kevin's Story

The night before my mom died, she looked in good spirits and I had no idea that tomorrow would be her last day. She told me that she really didn't want to go into the ground just yet, but then, she rolled over in her bed and said painfully, "I just can't go on like this another day." I replied tenderly, "You don't have to because we got some new medicine that should make you get better soon." I was getting ready to leave and she squeezed my fingers as usual, but this time, instead of squeezing tightly, her grip was limp. This freaked me out a bit but I figured she would still pull through cancer as she had done before.

I went to bed and woke up suddenly the next day at 4am. I felt something that was not the norm, for me. Could I have some weird sickness? I didn't feel that was possible since I was basically in good health, and I truly didn't think there was anything wrong with me. However, I had been having a fair amount of pain in my Achilles tendon. I decided to get out of bed and was prepared for my painful hobble into the bathroom, but this time, there was absolutely no pain. What could be going on here?

I walked around the house and I was feeling like someone had poured a bucket of bliss all over me. I was really calm, yet happy at the same time.

Even though I was healthy, getting up in the morning was not my favorite thing but today it was like I was renewed, recharged and refreshed to the max! I just wanted to lie down and absorb the vibes. I fell back to sleep for forty-five minutes until the phone rang. It was my mom's caregiver telling me to drive over immediately, that something was wrong with my mom's breathing. Normally, I would have bolted out of the house, driving like a maniac to be there, but today, instead of being out of control, (I thought) I would take a shower first. (I thought) I heard a voice say to me, "This is going to be a long day, so go eat something and don't panic." I downed some eggs and waffles, then sat and petted my dog for about five minutes. Thoughts came that I must bring overnight clothes to my mom's house, and I probably should be on my way now!

As I drove over to her house, I felt like I was being bathed in peace. My mom was still alive when I got there. I knew she wanted me there for her death. I was completely calm. I knew she was glad she did not die in a hospital. She started to breathe roughly so I gave her mouth to mouth resuscitation. The current caregiver had already called 911.

My sister, Alison, then entered the room and our mom died.

Alison and I exchanged our stories of the heavenly presence that encapsulated us for hours and hours. This presence remained with us the entire day. Every time in the next few days when we even so much as thought about the presence, it would come back to us.

As we relayed the story to father and our two sisters, they felt something greater had spoken to them, to calm them down.

We all feel we were spared from intense grieving. In the past, we all felt that when my mom died, we would all become (emotional) basket cases and (emotionally) fall apart. Because of the heavenly presence experiences, we are able to live our lives out in peace, with very little fear of death. We experienced some grief, but were not destroyed by it.

We felt that a higher power of some kind was in control and that everything is just the way it should be. It has now been a year since her death and during this time we all still feel that deep peace. With every thought of our dear mother we know that "everything is all right."

A GRANDFATHR'S VISIT

Glenda K. Rodger

It seems I've always been blessed with angels and also have been given the charge to help them from time to time.

The first experience I can remember took place when I was just nine years old. I was the youngest child in our family and was always the closest to each member of our family as well.

Growing up in Battle Creek, Michigan this had been a typical winter day for the Midwest - cold, overcast and dreary. My parents owned a business, a Rock Shop, and once a month they would have a "Rock Club" meeting. In the summertime these meetings would be held in the Rock Shop itself but, with heating costs and concerns during the winter months, these meetings would take place in the basement of our home, located just a few feet behind the business. I had remained upstairs because the meeting would last way past my bedtime.

It was a Tuesday night, about 7:30, when the telephone rang. I scurried to answer it before it made too much noise and disrupt the meeting. It was my Aunt Ruth, wanting to talk to my mother. We were not particularly close to any of our relatives from either my mother or father's side of the family, so a phone call at night was alarming all in itself. My mother immediately started crying and people from the meeting came to her side, to see what the news had been. I just watched. Mom seemed to be sobbing so much it took several minutes to find out the news. Her father, my only grandfather, had passed away. I had hardly any experience with death or dying. I started crying too, I remember thinking that is what I should be doing, so people would think I was a caring person.

I walked into my bedroom that I shared with my sister, Cheryl. There in the doorway was a figure of a man. Even though I had not been what I would call close to my grandfather, I knew it was my grandfather standing there. I was not frightened; I was very much at peace with the entire experience. Being a very shy and somewhat introverted child at the time this alone was remarkable. What would happen next would shape my life forever. I was sobbing; he looked at me, with a stern look and said to me "Glenda, you quit crying right now, you didn't even know me, what are you crying for?"

I told him I was crying because my mother was so sad with his passing.

He said in a much sterner voice than I had been used to "Stop it! Your mother needs you to be strong; you will always need to be there for her. She will always need you to watch out for her." With that he dissolved and was gone.

It would be many years before I would tell anyone of this experience. In numerous ways this experience with my grandfather helped me to be a better child to my parents. I never went through the rebellious years with either of my parents. At the time when most kids were giving their parents a very rough time, I seemed to be growing even closer to my mother.

In the late 1960's my Aunt Mary was diagnosed with breast cancer. Aunt Mary was a very short person with a chest that could have rivaled Dolly Parton. My aunt was also a very heavy smoker. My mother and I would go visit Aunt Mary in the hospital several nights a week after school. We lived out in the country, so these trips gave us lots of time to grow closer and for me to help mom with the grief she was feeling, seeing her favorite sister slowly dying a very painful death. Cancer treatments were not very advanced at this time and suffering, although never easy, was much worse back then. I remember seeing the look on Aunt Mary's face when she saw my mother, it would illuminate. Many times, I did not feel like going, to me it was sad knowing she was dying, but the strength came, it was not until much later that I realized where indeed this strength came from to help my mother.

It was my grandfather that gave me this strength to become my mother's protector.

After my father passed on, my mother, who still lived in Michigan, well over 2,000 miles away from me, suffered a severe depression. Mom would visit several times a year but it wasn't until I found out, after nearly twenty years of marriage, my husband, Lonnie and I were expecting our first child; that mom came to live with us. I had been Daddy's little girl for thirty-five years and never knew that my father repeatedly told my mother, "Glenda needs a little girl."

Not only have I been blessed with being there for my mother through her two bouts with breast and colon cancer, but also she has been there for me. Between my angelic mother, my grandfather, my father and my daughter, Angels of protection surround me.

OF BLACK ICE AND ILLNESS

Marysue Rivera

One frosty, cold winter's morning, when her three children were all younger than eight years old, my mother was driving to work. She wasn't happy about leaving her babies, but with Dad being laid off, there wasn't a choice. She did what she had to do for our family. To me, that's a sign she was an angel in and of itself. On this early, crisp and cold winter morning, she traveled from her house to her morning job, all alone. Her thoughts were on her children still snuggled in their warm beds. She told us she was thinking about us, and how it was getting close to the time for her girls to awake and get ready for school. Her baby boy would sleep a bit longer.

Suddenly, her car spun out of control, and hit a huge patch of unseen "black ice" on the road. The car spun around and started to head into the traffic behind her. She noticed that other cars were approaching her quickly. She knew they were about to hit the same unseen black ice, too, and that a big accident was likely to occur.

Frightened, my mom began to pray for help to bring the car back under control. All this happened within a split second, as if time had stopped. In that moment, she clearly heard her name spoken. The voice grabbed her attention, told her to take your foot off the brake pedal and spoke her name once again. Surprised, she looked to her right. Sitting next to her in the passenger seat was a young man with long, neat beautiful light hair. His face was calm, sweet, gentle and beautiful. He seemed to softly glow. She was suddenly at peace.

Seeing the young man, she felt calm when just seconds ago she was filled with fear. She immediately took her foot off the brake pedal, which unlocked the wheels of her car. Mom was then able to steer the car to the shoulder of the expressway, out of harm's way. The approaching cars flew by safely; the black ice was gone.

It's still amazing to think how the drivers who passed by her that day never knew that an angel protected them from the black ice. Mom looked back to the passenger seat after she watched the cars rush past, but her angel was gone.

Mom told us the story many times throughout our life. She knew without a doubt that she has seen her guardian angel and heard his voice in her car that day. Mom knew her angel had saved her from a horrendous car accident by his gentle, yet very necessary instruction to take her foot off the brake pedal. She believed her angel saved her life that day. Sometimes you just know things within your own soul and this was the knowledge given to her.

Many years later while fighting cancer, mom told me someone would peek at her on occasion. My mom was in a coma-like state for many days before passing. While I sat next to her hospital bed holding her hand, I felt overwhelmingly tired, heartbroken, weak and ill from fighting this long battle alongside her for so many months, one we eventually lost. While I sat vigilant at her bedside during her final days, she would sometimes briefly become conscious and would look up and over her right shoulder. I knew she saw someone. I kept trying to see what she was seeing.

It felt real to me and certainly it was real for her. She would continue to look up and over her shoulder over the next couple of days then turn and look at me and smile. Her peaceful, contented facial expression said everything to me. It brought strength to me. Words were not needed at this time for she could not speak.

I also saw that her face had an angelic, transparent glow lighting her cancer-stricken, sick face. It was an unbelievable sight to behold and much-needed for my grieving heart during such a difficult time. As she continued to look up and over her right shoulder I felt the angel's presence growing stronger each day as she grew weaker. I also felt more peaceful and calm in her final hours. I now knew for sure it was Mom's guardian angel, the one she first met in her car so many years ago.

Mom looked so content when she could see him near her. It was like she was seeing a loved one that she hadn't seen for a long time. I knew how much my mom loved life. I know how hard she fought to hang onto it. But now I knew she wanted to leave with her guardian angel. I lovingly whispered for her to go if she was ready.

When she passed, I know her beloved guardian angel was close and waiting for her. I knew that he would deliver her safely from her pain and suffering. Knowing this helped me cope with her passing. I also know what she now looks like, for I saw her transparent, angelic face before she left us. Beautiful, gentle, calm, and content. It is still amazing to me that in her final days, I felt mom's guardian angel close to me too, and that Mom was able to share him with me at that time.

Mom's guardian angel was not only there ministering to her, but was there to comfort, calm and strengthen me during that time as well. Mom's guardian angel gave me an understanding, beyond my own, during my time of need, through the loss and for many days after mom's passing. I loved my mother as much as was possible for a daughter to love anyone. I know now that my mom's angel was there checking on her in the hospital from behind the curtain, kept her safe many years ago in the car as a young mother and was there waiting for her when she passed over.

Today, I still believe my Mom and her guardian angel are close by my side. In the minutes just before my mother passed on that snowy winter's day, in November, a sudden thunder storm materialized. I thought this was unusual for that time of the year. While I watched the luminous lightening and felt the loud, intense thunder shake the walls and floor beneath me, I thought this was happening because a beautiful soul had just left this earth. As I write the final words of this story I can hear thunder coming in the distance from the west. A storm is quickly approaching.

Angel 16 / In the World of Business

There he is with that blue tie, projecting himself in to the world of business. As in all my angel images, the faces are completely, or partially, devoid of human features. It is my way of giving the images

a more universal feeling, and to make any physical connotations somewhat remote – not man, not woman, just pure spirit.

However, this angel's face is a flash of divine light. Isn't that what is needed in the world, and the world of business? Some of the other elements here – upper right-hand corner – the glaring animal head, symbolic of anger and greed, but his counterpart, the eagle (below the angel's chest) – freedom to fly toward love and clear, rational thinking. The lightening is a flash of God's omnipresent, all-pervading power and energy.

And the sun – well, everything revolves around the sun.

COOL ANGEL STAN

Ross Barbour

As I understand it the word "angel" meant messenger in early Hebrew writing. Angels didn't need halos or wings or flowing togas. That was added later. Those things were to add impact to the word "angel."

The "angel" who had the most impact on us, The Four Freshman, was Stan Kenton. Some of you who knew Stan are reading and smiling a wry smile at my calling Stan an "angel" because Stan had been known to be profane on occasion, but check this out…

We had been on the road a couple of years trying to keep up on all our expenses. We needed something good to happen. On March 20, 1950, Stan Kenton was brought by some disc jockeys to the Esquire Lounge in Dayton, Ohio. Our group was on-stage when he and three or four people arrived. We could SEE him. It was as though GOD had come in to listen!!! We sounded awful, but Stan heard what we might become, not what we were.

That night he arranged for us to record an audition tape to be sent to Capitol Records. By the time the record got to Hollywood, Stan planned to talk them into signing us to a contract.

We thought we were stars with a record contract, but the first two records didn't sell, hence Capitol dropped us. The third pair of songs we had recorded was "Tuxedo Junction" and "It's a Blue World."

When Stan found out we were dropped, he talked Capitol executives into making three copies of those songs and sending them to us. This was the summer of 1952, and the way they copied records was to play the record, and a blank disk at the same time, and the sound was transferred into the new grooves by a stick fastened to the two "pick-up-heads." Anyhow, we gave those disks to a disc jockey named Bob Murphy on WJBK Detroit (another angel). Murphy copied those records, and gave copies to the other disc jockeys in Detroit.

Within a week, both sides of the record were 'turntable hits" and we were not even signed to Capitol. Stan talked Capitol into re-signing us, and releasing it. Due to the success of that record Capitol let us choose the songs we did, and the way we did them. In the next six or seven years, we made successful musical records. Stan would check on us once in awhile and help us along.

Through it all, we couldn't believe he wanted to be that involved with us. He had a band on the road and worries of his own. He had adopted us as though we were his family. People would say to him, "you ought to record with the Four Freshman" and he would say, "they don't need my band and the band doesn't need them."

Later, though, we recorded one of the nights, in a month of one-niters with Stan's band, along with June Christy. That was in 1959, and in 1972 we recorded an album called "Live at Butler."

Through it all, from beginning to end, Stan wouldn't let us pay a penny for any of it. He wouldn't let us even give him a Christmas present.

The records with the band helped our career, but the biggest "help" was to have Stan Kenton pulling for us. All Stan had to do was to mention that he liked our group, and people made it a point to check us out.

Stan Kenton was the greatest leader of men I have ever met. We would have run into a brick wall without him. Early in our association with him, he said, "You guys have GOT to succeed...you're part of my ego." We never discussed quitting after he said that.

Stan Kenton was an angel for us, and for a hundred other musicians, groups and singers.

So you see, angels don't need halos, have to have wings or wear togas.

Angel 12
Of Overall Protective Blessings

Flashes of blue and yellow light encircle this angel, who looks directly at us - all symbols of protection on every rung of a holistic ladder. The two animals, painted within the body of this being, symbolize life on a planet where the norm seems to center around war, fear, anger, rage, irrational thinking and darkness, but up in that cloudless, starless, mid blue sky sits that lopsided moon that lights the way for God's love and protection.

BLESSINGS IN SPANISH

Edid Espinal

This event took place in the summer of 1991.

My friend, who I will call Rene, and I, were going to assist a gentleman, who was referred to her by her husband, Joaquin. This man, who we will call Tom, was going through some very difficult issues – mental, physical and emotional. Joaquin had talked to Rene, in the context, which he felt I could be of some assistance to Tom. I had done spiritual readings, and he felt confident that I could help.

We planned to set up a date and Rene and I were going to meet Tom at his place of business. He was the owner of a restaurant/lounge/bar located in Spanish Harlem on Broadway. I was driving my vehicle, and Rene was the passenger. When we arrived Joaquin and Tom were waiting for us outside the lounge.

As we arrived, we pulled up on the corner where they were waiting, and they approached the car. Joaquin then introduced Tom to me. The intro took place as Tom was peering into the auto from the passenger side. As the introduction took place, Tom looked at me like I was an alien from another planet, and had this puzzled look, like, 'what the hell is she going to do for me?'

We told them that we were going to look for parking, and, at that point, Tom took Joaquin aside and said something to him. The result of that short meeting was a request from Tom for us to come back another time. Rene and I were looking at each other kind of in states of confusion and disbelief. We had no idea what was going on; after all, we had stayed up most of the previous night, seriously and sincerely preparing for this meeting in which we could be of service to this gentleman.

At the moment he said this, we could only ask, "What happened? Why are you changing your mind, what's going on?" It was obvious that he was giving us some excuse, like 'something has come up.' We knew this was only an excuse. This really got my dander up; after all the energy we put into preparing for helping someone, and this is the way he treats us!

We were still sitting in the car, analyzing all this, and finally, we said, "Okay" and I started driving away. We were headed north on Broadway toward 155th street, where I was going to take the highway back home. Before I approached 155th street, I kept on hearing the honking of another vehicle. I was ignoring this sound, just thinking it was a driver in some kind of rushed state. The horn kept honking, and I kind of silently stated something like, 'what the hell do you want me to do??!!?' It was bumper -to- bumper traffic, and we were in this kind of interesting state of confusion. This vehicle was to the left of me; however, I did my best to ignore him. He kept on honking, and then started to cut me off, not aggressively, but he pulled in front of me to get to the right side of the road. He was now closest to my passenger side. I saw, for the first time, that his vehicle is a taxi, not the Yellow Cab variety, but a black, self-owned vehicle, what is known in the area, as a 'Gypsy Cab.' Now, he is looking at us and signaling with his hand, like 'roll down your window.' He wanted to tell us something. I said, "Rene, roll down the window and let's see what he wants."

We rolled down the window, and Rene signaled with her hand, like, 'What do you want?' He starts pointing to me, and in a very animated way says the following, in Spanish: "I want to talk to HER," meaning me. As this is all taking place, I'm still driving, and he loudly says the following, still in Spanish: "I'm Saint Michael, and I'm here to protect you for the next twenty years."

Now, let's stop here for a moment. I know that many readers of this story are going to have the reaction, with their eyes rolled up, like, 'another lunatic who thinks he's Saint Michael. There are also probably three hundred people in New York who think they are Jesus and six of them can prove it.' And I would say, if that's all there was to it I might be in agreement with them. However, here's the rest of the story.

As I said, we were in the midst of the morning rush hour on one of the major streets in Spanish Harlem, and after this exclamation, it was as if a heavenly event had taken place. As Rene and I were trying to figure out his statement, within a few seconds the taxi was gone, and the intense traffic that had been there moments before, was flowing, as if in a dream state. However, the main result of this angelic event was the realization that the meeting I was really preparing for was not with Tom, but for an encounter with the Archangel Michael, who spoke to me from a taxicab, in the 20th Century.

Within a few moments every bit of negative emotions, bitterness, confusion and irrational thoughts aimed at Tom were gone and I was in a state of love, bliss and joy.

And let me just add the following interesting synchronicity: Rene was a devotee of Archangel Michael, and she and I would often get together for spiritual discussions centering around God, angels, prayer, and generally attaining more awareness in living our lives on the highest levels of consciousness we could attain.

PARTY IN PARADISE

Bill Newell

I was at the 1977 Thanksgiving skydiving meet at Zephyrhills, near Tampa, Florida when Jim "Whitey" Whiting told me he was planning a New Year's Party in Paradise, skydiving adventure in Hawaii and asked if I'd like to attend and write an article about it for our Star Crest Magazine.

Free room and board for a week sounded good to me, plus I'd always wanted to go to Hawaii. Lots of my friends had already been several times, and at 36, time was ticking.

In a book I was reading on the flight over I was intrigued by the part that said earthbound and demon spirits resided in the depths of the earth. And the Mariana Trench, one of the deepest places in the ocean had an abnormal amount of paranormal activity and mysterious disappearances on its surface.

The Party in Paradise was held on Oahu's North Shore. Dillingham Airfield was where the skydiving was taking place, and about a mile farther west just before the paved road ended at Kaena Point was Camp Erdman where we skydivers were housed.

Camp Erdman – the skydivers called it Camp Wierdman – was a YMCA camp with a huge recreation hall and swimming pool right on the beach. Directly across the road were the cabins and right behind the cabins, rugged green mountains rose steeply to a couple of thousand feet. The scenery was fantastic.

The skydivers were sharing the recreation hall with middle school Japanese students during the day. I could sense the culture contrast, as did the Japanese instructors, but the skydivers seemed oblivious. As the Japanese kids were singing Disney type songs like "It's A Small, Small World," on the first floor, heavy metal music blared from the P.A. speakers in the chow hall on the second floor where the skydivers ate, drank and partied. There were some concerned looks from the Japanese instructors, but they never said anything.

All the cabins but one were full with skydivers from various parts of the mainland. Most groups from a certain place were housed together. I missed my original flight and arrived a day late, so I got the empty cabin. That was a good thing in that I had privacy and wouldn't be kept awake by a bunch of rowdy skydivers wanting to party all night.

About the third night we were having a party on the beach with a bon fire under the palm trees. I had downed a few beers when another late-comer showed up. He had just flown in from Washington State to meet his sister who was already there. This guy – I'll call him Don - was very loud and brassy. He was running around shouting "So this is the party in paradise, huh? Well let's get down and party!"

Awhile later I fell off the log I was sitting on. This generated a lot of laughs because at the time I was considered to be pretty hard core. I decided it was time to pack it in before I embarrassed myself any further, so I bid goodnight amid hoots and howls' and made it back to my cabin.

Here's where things got interesting. I was feeling truly euphoric, being in Hawaii, and as I lay on my bunk next to the louvered glass windows I could hear the surf as a continuous roar. Not like the California surf, where it ebbs, crescendos, splashes and hisses, but a continuous roar. I lapsed into a semiconscious state as the roar of the surf transcended into the most beautiful and intricate drumming I'd ever heard. I've been a conga drummer since my teens and I'd never heard anything that rhythmic. I was unfamiliar with those rhythms and couldn't play them at the time, so why was I hearing them in my head?

I snapped out of my trance and back came the roar of the waves. I thought, "Wow that was great. Let's see if I can do that again." Sure enough, I was able to replace the roar of the breaking waves with the drums. After about the third time, I began to get a little flippant, thinking "Hey, I can do this any time I want."

Just then, right through the wall facing the mountains marched 5 or 6 Hawaiian warriors from a time past. They were in full color, slightly transparent, had spears and shields and looked angry, although they didn't seem demonic. As they glided past my bunk their feet were moving but didn't appear to be touching the floor. They paused briefly and one of them looked at me before they continued on out through the opposite wall.

I rose up in my bunk and exclaimed aloud. "This can't be real!!" As soon as I said that, a gust blew in from the louvered windows and kicked up a grayish whirlwind blowing dust and debris at the foot of my bunk. Seeing this psychic phenomena backed up by a physical manifestation convinced me that it was real, and I cried "Lord, help me," as I pulled the blanket over my head. As soon as I said "Lord, help me," the whirlwind dissipated and blew out the window. I was scared and lay there wondering what had just happened. I hadn't been to church in years and wasn't in the habit of calling on God. But it worked.

Did calling on God when I was scared enable an angel to intervene and protect me? I believe so. Early in life I sensed an image of a dual self. I felt something was with me most of the time; my other self. In near misses or accidents it seemed to take over and I was merely a spectator.

Enter Don, who as a late-comer also got a bunk in the spare cabin. His bunk was on the other side of the room from mine and in between us was the bathroom and shower, so even though I couldn't see him I could hear him. It was about 2:00 am and Don, who had previously been running around crowing party, party, party, was tossing and turning in his bunk, retching and moaning that something was after him and he wanted to go back home. He'd been in Hawaii for the first time for only a few hours.

By that time I became aware of what was going on; the spirit's were harassing Don. He couldn't see them as I had, but he was feeling them. I went over to his bunk and said "Take it easy, partner. You'll be OK, you just have island fever." But he insisted, "No, I got to get out of here, now! Get Whitey up and get me to the airport!"

So that's what I did, at 3:00 am. Whitey was in his private cabin with his girlfriend and he didn't like it. But Don was stressing so bad, Whitey decided it was better to drive him to the Honolulu airport than to have him running around freaking out at the Party in Paradise. Don arrived about 6:00 pm and was on his way home by 4:00 am. Ten hours in "paradise".

I cautiously told a couple of skydivers the next day about my experience and their reaction was that I had too much to drink. However, when I asked a few native Hawaiians, they told me that spirit sightings were not uncommon in the islands, and that other people (mainly locals) had seen similar scenarios in the same area. One Hawaiian asked if the spirit had looked at me. When I answered yes, but briefly, he looked concerned and said "If they look at you, the legend says that you will die." Well I didn't die, but a whole plane load of skydivers who were at that Party in Paradise died three years later on December 6th, 1981.

Whitey and some of his local skydiving friends – most of whom had attended the Party in Paradise boogies in '78', '79 and '80 - were to make an exhibition jump into a football game at Aloha Stadium next to Pearl Harbor.

The 12 place Twin Beech stalled in a tight turn over the stadium at a low altitude - rolled and crashed upside down next to the Arizona Memorial in Pearl Harbor. Only one guy bailed out in time to survive. The rest were all killed, including Whitey, sitting in the front seat with the pilot.

On my last visit there in '84, I overheard some of the guys at a party talking about how ironic that a month or so before the crash, Whitey had made a mock recording, with sound affects and screams, of the Beech crashing in the ocean off Kaena Point. They played it for me. It was chilling and prophetic.

My mind flashed back to the first Party in Paradise in 1978, when I was walking along a road by the beach and Whitey picked me up in his car. When I got in, he said, “Hi Newell, how does it feel to be dead?” I replied rather irritated, “What the hell are you talking about? I’m not dead!” He said, “Oh yes you are, but you don’t know it. Look around. You’re in paradise!”

My angel of protection has intervened for me countless times since then.

LOVE REVEALED

Anonymous

I was eighteen years old and in a bad relationship with my boyfriend. He used to be the man of my dreams, but then something happened – who knows what? He had digressed into drugs, alcohol and also became one of the non-working class. We used to live together but, by the grace of God, I was able to separate myself enough from him that we both got our own apartments. However, emotions don’t drop off immediately and I still went over to his place, visited and, at times, spent the night.

It was horrifying to see how he kept his place; it was an absolute mess. The health department should have been called in. The smell of the place was horrid. Nothing I could say could change him to clean, go to work, or get off of drugs and alcohol.

People told me to just ‘drop him’ but I could not do so. Memories of how he used to be – good, caring, working and sober – prevented this action. I wanted who ‘he really is’ back, and I was willing to hang in there until that was accomplished.

One night, while visiting his place, I decided to go into the bedroom and meditate. I had previously learned some meditation techniques and was trying to make it a regular practice. I was told that one has to really 'go deep' to get the full benefit of the practice. I was also told you have to totally concentrate on the breath or thought of God or both, and I was willing to just dive into this 'meditation realm' to it's fullest because, what I was experiencing on planet earth, was just horrible.

I sat in a chair around 8pm. The lights were out and I closed my eyes. I sat as still as one can possibly sit, and I focused on my 'third eye' (between my two physical eyes), and I literally poured my heart out to God to 'PLEASE REVEAL THYSELF! PLEASE TAKE ME, AND SHOW ME WHAT TRUE LOVE IS! FROM THE SOURCE, FROM GOD, I MUST KNOW, AND I MUST KNOW, RIGHT NOW!'

My concentration was total…and then something began to happen. My feet, hands and third eye became hot. I opened my eyes and I had changed into a white angelic light, and the peace and love in the room was everywhere as the white light expanded itself. I could not even see my physical body anymore. It was as if I became an angel of light. Light was everywhere. It was ethereal..like I was floating.

Immediately my boyfriend opened the door because he felt it from the other room, and he saw it as well. He saw that I was now 'light.' We both stood there for what seemed like an eternity, not knowing what to do. I motioned for him to go away, so I could continue in the envelopment of this sacred energy.

I then decided to get up, go outside, and walk around. I had returned to the physical body, and the white light disappeared. However, what stayed with me was the INCREDIBLE LOVE I FELT FOR EVERYONE….ABSOLUTELY EVERYONE! I wanted to go out and hug everyone and tell the world that all is well, and God is accessible, and that Supreme Consciousness, that Supreme Joy and Bliss is there, now, in the present!

My body, mind and soul stayed in that pure God Energy, but I decided to force myself to sleep, just in case, since I had to go to work the next day.

Within about a month, I never saw my boyfriend again. On his own, he decided to move far away, which was a blessing, since I could not cut that cord on my own.

Although I felt true love for him, not all who love should be together in a relationship. So, this is a story of love and protection. I was protected, and hoped that the love and light I became, through my experience, would help awaken him to new, positive roles he would live out - on this earthly abode.

FROM TRAGEDY TO GLORY

Clara L. Peck

I was born on Christmas Eve into a family of three other children including twins just over a year old. The year was 1922 and times were good for my family before the depression. My life would change dramatically on February 24, 1924 however, when I was just fourteen months old. My Aunt Bee, who helped my mother with all of us children, (she was only twelve or so herself) took my oldest brother out sledding, leaving the twins and I alone; mother was busy upstairs. The twins picked up the Sunday paper and put it into the open fireplace. It immediately caught on fire and they quickly pulled it out and ran and hid. Seeing the bright and pretty flame I walked toward it and fell head first into the inferno. My father, who had been outdoors working, came running in to see what all the commotion was about. There I lay, the flames were out, but I lay there still, almost lifeless. My father called the old country doctor who arrived in quick order by horse and buggy. The doctor did not give me much chance. I had raised my arm up over my forehead and that had protected my eyes at least. Then the doctor told my parents what they already knew, that there was no hospital in our rural Ohio town and it would not be wise to move me anyway. He wrapped me in gauze and told my parents that he would be back the next day to check on me.

The next day he came, as he did everyday, for several weeks. He told my parents one day that if I had been burnt one single inch more anywhere on my body I would not have survived. He was a very nice old country doctor with this magical salve he would rub on my burns and tell me I could grow up and shave like my dad if I would put this on every day. However, months later he stopped coming.

A few years later the depression hit and times were rough for everyone. One day all of us children had more toys than we knew what to do with, and the very next day, nothing at all. My mother thought because of my pathetic looks, (I had three holes around my mouth that would drain continuously), people would take pity on me so I would get to be the lucky one to stand in the lines for the ration coupons. I was never my mother's favorite child and it almost seemed to me growing up that she often resented the fact that I had lived.

I quit school shortly after starting high school. I was needed at home to take care of the younger children and I was tired. I was a scared, young, innocent child, and tired of the ridicule and the mean things that were aimed at me.

My older sister and I ended up moving to Michigan and taking our younger sisters with us to raise. While working at a local factory I met the man of my dreams. He looked at me and saw what was behind the face; this was real love. When my mother found out that he had proposed to me she was furious. I was the "ugly" child; I should not be the first to get married. Getting married is exactly what I did, much to her dismay.

I've had several close calls in my life. Once in 1950 I was scheduled for exploratory surgery. I was taken early because of a cancellation, only to find out that I would have died if they had waited for the "scheduled" surgery.

My guardian angel once again came in a very unusual way in 1991. My husband lay in the hospital with a heart attack; we later found out he was in the advanced stages of Alzheimer's disease, and his physician, one day after examining him, demanded I make an appointment for myself. I did and was diagnosed with malignant colon cancer. Luckily it was caught in the early stages.

Thanks to my guardian angels I am a survivor and have been blessed with a loving husband and four healthy happy children, many grand and great-grand children.

A LITTLE BIT OF OBITUARY HUMOR

Glenda K. Rodger

Mom took her last breath, after suffering what seemed to me unimaginable pain from her adventures with breast cancer, on a very pretty summer Saturday afternoon, surrounded by her four loving children and one of her many loving grand-daughters. The next day everyone would be leaving, and my daughter, my husband and I would be alone in the house. How lonely it seemed; mom had lived with us for sixteen years and now she was gone, or so I thought, as I delved into self-pity. I desperately wanted her back for at least one last long hug, or the loving opportunity to run my hands through her extra soft beautiful white hair. However, my daughter and I planned her "celebration of life" services that would keep us busy for the days ahead.

A few days went by and, in the middle of one night, my husband woke me up, and said I needed to take him to the hospital, right now! He was bent over and screaming in pain. I did not want my fifteen-year old daughter to wake up to an empty house, since she had just lost her grandma a couple days previous, so I went into her room and ever so gently woke her up and explained what was happening. I told her not to worry. 'You know how men are with pain,' and proceeded to take my husband the twenty-five miles to the nearest hospital. Several hours went by and the doctors had his pain under control, and were running all kinds of tests to locate the nature of the problem. I told him I felt the need to go home and check on our daughter; he was being well taken care of and there was really nothing more I could do more for him at that point. I get in the car, hopped onto the freeway, and, once again, got struck with the overwhelming urge to cry and indulge myself in self-pity. 'How much can one person take,' I said to myself; 'I lose my mom, my husband is in the emergency room, and my daughter is all by herself.' As if she were sitting in the passenger seat of my car I heard my mother laughing, loudly and hysterically. I said, "Mom what's up?" She said "Glen, go figure." I said, "Go figure what mom?" She said, "The one day I don't read the obituaries my name is there!"

When I arrived home the first thing I did was look at the newspaper; sure enough mom's obituary was in the paper that day.

Somehow I knew I had another guardian angel letting me know we would get through everything - together.

PRESENCE OF INTENTION

Wil Kinsley

My Mother had recently passed, and I was spending a lot of time putting together an on-line photo album; creating a story of happier times in her life through the pictures of her vacations here in Los Angeles with me. As I would retouch and frame old photos of her as a little girl, perhaps I was strengthening a bond or created a psychic link that helped connect a way for my Mom to come through.

It was around 5:30 in the morning and I woke up to my body convulsing to an enormous energy rush. I have no memory of anything that might have immediately precipitated this, all I know is my body was arching and this astonishing flow of unlimited goodwill and energy was coursing into me. I do not remember if my eyes were opened or not, I only know that it wouldn't have been necessary to see out of them to know precisely where everything in that room was.

I will try my best to describe it knowing I can never do it adequate justice but I have to try. The 'energy' was a physical, living, limitless, presence of Intention. It had Purpose. It had Being. It was Joy In Creating. You couldn't give it a name, because it was just too big, too beyond anything I could possibly hold in or outside of my mind and say, "You are that!" I knew without any doubt that this 'Feeling', understood me, more than I could ever hope to know it or myself. This Power has instantly risen up inside of me as if it were a fountain suddenly turned on full throttle, but as I shot from 0 to (actually I cannot think of a reference), I found myself in a place of incredible stability. All the Power and Energy and Purpose was there, holding, suspending and sustaining me; but it never once fluctuated or was at any point 'Less Than'. I have never had such a comprehensive appreciation of what 'Consistency' is. I was in a space that knew itself to be 'Real', and never had been anything else. There was no gravity. Nothing was pulling on me. This is perhaps my most singular impression of awe. You can't really imagine what the sensation of no gravity is, until it's gone. All ties are broken, you are free of this burden of heaviness that hooks into every part of you and relentlessly pulls and sets upon you, everyday of your life. I am so grateful for that gift of floating free and weightless for those few minutes.

This Power rushing through you creates an enormous amount of inner energy but it's not like 'I have to jump up and start ironing clothes energy', it fills you with peace and the knowing that there is no time here to fill. That's when I became more aware of the 'voice' that had been there from the beginning. Not really a voice, but the 'Feeling' of one. It's message was, "Everything is OK." "Everything is just fine." "Everything is just the way as it should be." And I knew it to be my Mom.

How long I really lay there and let it wash over me I'm going to say 4 minutes. But I'm sure that's a little subjective. I was able to reach a compromise by imagining myself being healed. I am uncomfortable when a lot of attention is being paid to me and this was off the chart! Then there is that part of you that wants to jump up and tell someone. Anyone. Everyone! But by agreeing to be healed I was able to lie still and let this amazing experience into my life and for those few precious minutes I communed with my Mother's Miracle.

Best intentions aside and me being me, I had to eventually jump out of bed and tell someone what had happened. The sensation gently vanished as I sat up and ran into the next room to tell my partner. John was an Intensive Care nurse and his hours were horrendous so it was not unusual that he would be up and at the computer at this time in the morning. Like a kid on Christmas morning I blurted out and sputtered my way through what had just happened to me. To Me! I left nothing out. The excitement of trying to relive it was really nothing compared to what had just happened, but I was certainly giving it my best, so maybe that's why I didn't see it coming.

Now I know how people who claim they've seen UFO's must feel. He didn't believe me. Not even enough to ask me a question about it. The look on his face as he rolled his eyes, shook his head that he had been so bothered by my silly ranting and then swivelled around in his chair and got back to what was really important.

I guess my point is, maybe it really is about your own experience of what is real and purposeful in YOUR life. You can't depend upon others validating your experience and making it even more wonderful; compounding the 'wonder of it all' as you will... I know this to be true. It happened to me, but I've sat on this story until I came across this collection of angel stories, and at last my words have found a page.

And if anyone is wondering, John and I went our separate ways and a year ago I started a new spiritual journey with my partner here in Austin.

NIGHT OF FORGIVENESS

Angela Taylor

I will never forget this first time angel experience my friends and I had together, back when we all had just graduated from high school.

I was living on my own, in a small apartment with my boyfriend, Chris. My best girlfriend Linda stayed with us from time to time. Life was rather dramatic, with lots of ups and downs, as it tends to be for many teens. I had recently broken away from my parents; from their religion, and I had become a vegetarian and started seeing holistic doctors. In short, I was breaking away from them in their role as parents. They had a very difficult time accepting this 'breaking-away' behavior, and showed their unified displeasure in a way that I would describe as "hating this", "hating that", "hating my boyfriend" and "best friend" as well. In fact, the word "disowning me" had come up a lot in their conversations. And this often happened when I was around them.

Although I liked my freedom from parental control, I had a two-bit job and it was hard to make ends meet, but wanting to be on my own, and make my own decisions, became the priority in my life. This basically involved decisions in job areas, religion, food choices, health, etc. Chris, Linda and I were reading books revolving around many areas of the metaphysical world; one of our main life interests was trying to connect to a religion that we resonated with on the highest spiritual levels.

One evening, while we - Chris, Linda and I - were all seated in the living room, we started talking about religion. Somehow that led us to 'confessing our sins' to each other. From the deepest depths of our hearts and souls we poured out the worst things we had done and were asking God, the Universe, whoever, to PLEASE forgive us. The three of us were so deeply sorry. As I look back, there is a little humor connected with this, as we hadn't committed terrible sins by any means. We hadn't exactly robbed any banks, or hurt anyone, but we were young, serious and sincere, and we were truly sorry about some things we did, or didn't do, in life.

Suddenly, out of the blue, from up above, a force field of moving white light descended into our heads, into our third eye (above the eyebrows, in the middle of the forehead – sometimes called 'The Spiritual Eye'), and down to our hearts. The fan in the room that was on started going crazy and blowing wind everywhere and the light seemed to be moving and growing larger and larger. The moving white light, and the wind, filled the entire room and we all felt like we were being forgiven completely.

Still, in that moment in time, we didn't know what to do next. Should we sit there and let it keep happening? Do we get up? We were completely stunned. I then opened the front door to see if all of this was happening outside and yes, the white light seemed to expand even to the parking lot area. Then within about five to ten minutes it all dissipated and disappeared. I believe it was a huge blessing from our guardian angels absolving us for past mistakes. This incredible experience had a tremendous impact. All of us felt we would be on a new road in life.

After that experience, I found the religion I have now been on for the past thirty-five years, and for which I am eternally grateful.

I will never forget what the power of discharging our thoughts and feelings can do, and that our confessions are truly being heard by our angels.

Alphabetical Listings of Stories

Alphabetical Listings of Stories

Alphabetical Listings of Writers

Alphabetical Listings of Writers

CPSIA information can be obtained at www.ICGtesting.com
224749LV00002B/112/P

9 780982 787724